Kelly turned to face her husband.

Just as she'd feared—he looked movie-star gorgeous, and it took her breath away. Simon's stylish black dinner suit and classic black tie radiated good taste and probably cost more than Kelly made in a month. He leaned in to place a kiss on her cheek and Kelly moved to accept it, catching a waft of expensive aftershave.

"You look beautiful, Kell," Simon said, his subdued voice as disarming as his good looks.

"So do you."

A soft smile touched his mouth. He was so beautiful. So elegant. So self-assured.

Who is this man? Kelly wondered as she tried to relate the sensations she was experiencing to those she'd felt so many years before. And found that she could not. This was different. This was adult. And this was fast spinning out of her control.

"How long have you been waiting?" he asked, his voice a caress in the dreamy darkness.

For you? For five long, lonely years.

"Not long," she said, her voice barely a whisper.

D0018193

**For better, for worse...these marriages
were meant to last!**

They've already said "I do," but what happens
when their promise to love, honor and
cherish is put to the test?

Emotions run high as husbands and wives discover
how precious—and fragile—their wedding vows are...
but their love will keep them together—forever!

Ally Blake worked in retail, danced on television
and acted in friends' short films until the writing bug
could no longer be ignored. And as her mother had
read romance novels ever since Ally was a baby, the
aspiration to write for Harlequin had been almost bred
into her. Ally married her gorgeous husband, Mark,
in Las Vegas (no Elvis in sight, thank you very much),
and they live in beautiful Melbourne, Australia. Her
husband cooks, he cleans and he's the love of her
life. How's that for a hero?

Books by Ally Blake

HARLEQUIN ROMANCE®
3782—THE WEDDING WISH
3802—MARRIAGE MATERIAL

MARRIAGE
MAKE-OVER

Ally Blake

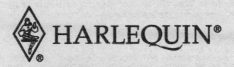

TORONTO • NEW YORK • LONDON
AMSTERDAM • PARIS • SYDNEY • HAMBURG
STOCKHOLM • ATHENS • TOKYO • MILAN • MADRID
PRAGUE • WARSAW • BUDAPEST • AUCKLAND

To Harry's real life skipper, my little sister Suze, a girl who can see the bright side of any situation and thus makes life that much brighter for the rest of us.

ISBN 0-373-03830-5

MARRIAGE MAKE-OVER

First North American Publication 2005.

www.eHarlequin.com

Printed in U.S.A.

CHAPTER ONE

KELLYISM:
SO YOU WANT TO BE A 'SINGLE AND LOVING IT!' GIRL?
BE RESOLUTE. BE FEARLESS. BE HEARD!

'KELLY ROCKFORD. Babe. You're a hit!'

That was the kind of talk Kelly had heard only in her dreams. But there she was, sitting at Editor-in-Chief Maya Rampling's desk at *Fresh* magazine, hearing those glorious words for real.

Maya's talon-tipped finger tapped the draft of Kelly's latest magazine column, which lay on her desk. 'This is your best effort yet. Your column has really touched a nerve. Barely a month on and we are getting more mail for you than any other regular writer. As such I would like to offer you a freelance contract here at *Fresh*.'

Single and Loving It!, her pride and joy, her week-by-week column about how to be a happy single, was now her ticket out of writing bridal announcements and obituaries in the local rags! *And* she would be able to pay the rent on time. Her heart almost burst at the thought.

A dead-straight strand of cocoa-coloured fringe slipped from Kelly's straining ponytail and swung before her eyes. She had to fight the urge to blow the offending lock away as, knowing her luck, she would blow a raspberry rather than the smooth, perfectly aimed puff of air she would prefer. And she wanted to remember herself in this perfect moment as the epitome of cool. Well, maybe not cool so much as *not* blowing a raspberry at an inopportune moment. She could hope for at least that much.

'We will offer you a three-month contract,' Maya continued in the face of Kelly's strained silence. 'Work at your own pace. Here or at home. Just as long as your copy is on my desk every Monday afternoon at five, and the work and the reader response stay on track, you will be a welcome and regular member of the *Fresh* family. Come on, I'll show you to your work-station.'

Maya stood and led the way. In desperate relief Kelly raked her hand over her hair, tucking the fringe back in place. There. Cool Kelly held her ground.

And then she saw her work-station and had to choke back a gasp of splendiferous happiness. It was her very own tiny three-walled cubicle amongst a dozen other tiny three-walled cubicles. The desk was so sparse it reminded her of the first day of school when every new pencil was sharpened and no book was dog-eared or scratched. The work-station housed a corkboard, a filing cabinet, a phone, an assortment of stationery and a computer, which was turned on and opened to a fresh, hopeful Word file.

Kelly took off her faded denim jacket and fluffy pink scarf and hung them over the back of her very own bouncy office chair. She took a seat, swung back and forth and imagined dozens of happy snaps plastered over her corkboard, her 'I Hate Working Wednesdays, They Really Cut Into My Weekends' mug resting amidst a ring of stale coffee, and assorted funky knick-knacks balanced atop her monitor. Yep. This was her dream come true.

'So how does that all sound?' Maya asked.

As if the angels were singing her song!

'Sounds fine, thanks,' cool Kelly responded.

'Great. First things first: your next column. You have touched on something very deep and given it a voice. So, of course, I want you to hit that vein deeper and deeper every week. Our female readers love you so, in my infinite wisdom, I have decided reader feedback will become a huge part of your page. We will start with a whammy. In amongst your legion of new fans, there was one reader who was not convinced.'

'Just one?' *Good one, Kelly, real cool and confident!*

Maya smiled indulgently, her sharp, preternaturally smooth face breaking into a zillion telling wrinkles at the unfamiliar movement. 'One juicy one who made an interesting point. So maybe you could respond to this beauty in next week's issue.'

Maya flicked a one-page letter onto Kelly's desk as she left. 'Have fun, and welcome to the *Fresh* family.'

Have fun? This was turning out to be the best day of her life! The best she cared to remember, anyway. She now had a real job doing something she utterly loved, her very own quasi-office with her very own bouncy chair, and lastly a real pay-packet, a *regular* pay-packet. How she wished she could have stapled her mother to the wall to have listened to everything Maya had said. Then her life would be perfect.

Kelly picked up the letter. She unconsciously fiddled with the corners of the folded piece of baby-blue paper.

Truth be told, Kelly was surprised there was only one not convinced. The *Single and Loving It!* idea had come about around a month before after a Saturday Night Cocktails session with her flatmate, racy Gracie, and her landlady, classy Cara, during which they had bitched and moaned about their conglomerate of ex-boyfriends. How they'd thrown every ounce of their energy into the relationships whereas the guys had seen them as a step above cricket practice but not so important as Mum's home cooking. *Was that love?* they had asked. *Was that as good as it could be?*

So *Single and Loving It!* was born. Kelly had written her first attempt the minute she had trudged home. It had been three a.m., there had been no coffee in the cupboard, as she had not been able to afford it, so she had plied herself with chicken Cup-a-Soup. She had sold the story to *Fresh* within the week and had been writing weekly follow-ups ever since.

She glanced down at the letter. In her fidgeting hands lay the first piece of fan mail she had ever received. Well, except for that one old guy who once had been determined she was the only one he would allow to write his obituary (first job after uni—bad office, bad pay, bad news).

She rubbed her fingers over the fine paper, memorising the touch. She took a deep breath and dived in.

Dear Kelly
Men and women are meant to be attracted, but not for ever, you say. They come together to fill in space, time, and the void left by their parents, you say. Well, dear Kelly, I don't believe a word of it.

I believe you are a woman who has loved and loved deeply. I believe you have convinced yourself there is no such thing as love so that you do not have to feel you have failed.

And the thing is, dear Kelly, I believe love is alive and well out there. Especially for you. You just have to be willing to lose yourself to find it.
Simon of St Kilda.

Kelly dropped the letter to the table as though it had scorched her fingers. She hastily looked over her shoulder to make sure no one had seen the words on the paper, the words she wanted nobody else to believe, as no more potentially damaging words had ever been written.

How did the writer know? How? Then out of the red mist before her eyes swam the most telling part of the read. She picked up the letter between two fingers and re-read the name at the bottom of the page.

Simon of St Kilda.

No, it couldn't be!

If she thought her fingers felt hot before, that was nothing compared with the storm of heat that radiated from her flushed face at those words.

Kelly knew a Simon, but that had been a lifetime ago. And the last she'd heard he lived in Fremantle, on the other side of Australia. Not in Melbourne and certainly not in St Kilda. Not in the same suburb as her.

The letter was typewritten, including the name, so that was no clue. She sniffed at it. It smelled like paper and not like a wood fire at the beach, which was the smell that always reminded her of Simon. She looked closely, checking to see if any letters sat higher than any others. What that would prove she had no idea, but it was the first thing they looked for in any good detective movie.

Who was she kidding? She did not need any fancy fingerprint kit to know that the Simon she knew wrote the letter. She could feel the timbre of his voice in every syllable. She knew his language so well it made the hairs on the back of her neck tingle as though he had whispered the words in her ear.

Simon of St Kilda was Simon Coleman. Her Simon Coleman, whom she had not heard from in five years. Since a week after her eighteenth birthday. Since, for some unknown reason that she had never been able to figure out, he had been spooked and sent dashing from her, never to return.

But now he was back. And writing to her of love.

Her face burned, not from embarrassment but from a deep and abiding anger. How dare he even write the words much less about her? He was the last one to accuse her of any denial when it came to her feelings. She had always made her feelings known without restraint. She had poured them out in print to millions, had she not?

'So what do you think?' Maya asked as she passed by Kelly's desk.

Kelly flinched so violently her chair continued bouncing for several seconds. 'Hmm?'

'The letter,' Maya said. 'Do you think you can explain yourself to him? Can you tell that guy where to go?'

Ooh, yeah. And you wouldn't even have to pay me to do it.

'I would be happy to. But didn't you say there were nice ones? Lots of nice ones? Ones that agreed with me? Ones that said I was brilliant and should be bronzed this minute?'

'Sure. But who wants to read those when you've got this guy just asking to be put in his place?'

Me! I do!

Kelly shrugged. 'Nobody, I guess.'

'Exactly. So, dear Kelly,' Maya said with a twinkle in her wise eyes, 'write me a blinder. I want it bigger and better and more controversial. I want Simon of St Kilda in the picture.'

Ha! Give me a time machine and I'll give you my life with Simon in the picture.

Maya patted her on the shoulder and left to rouse another writer.

What did he want? Why was he back? And how on earth could she keep herself together if and when she saw him? The mental image of her wringing his beautiful neck gave her a small thrill.

She shuffled the computer mouse onto the internet icon, looked up the local phone directory, and found only one S. Coleman listed in St Kilda. Her hand shaking, she picked up the handset of her very own phone that only minutes before had given her such ridiculous pleasure, and dialled.

Because even if Maya had not insisted, she would still have to see him.

He was her husband.

Kelly stood on the sidewalk with feet of lead. Her eyes were locked on the third storey of the swanky St Kilda apartment building. The window was open, and white gauzy curtains flapped in the seaside breeze. Somebody was home. And it had to be S. Coleman.

After dialling and hanging up the phone several times that morning she had given up on the idea of calling. She had to *see* that it was him. She had to meet him face to face.

So, first things first, she had spent *hours* making her work-station homey before finally making her way to the address written on the piece of paper clasped in her clammy hand. It wasn't cowardice that made her delay this moment. The decorating project was imperative. After all, a happy working environment did a happy worker make!

Now, in the late afternoon, devoid of denim jacket and scarf, which she had thoughtlessly left on the back of her chair, she felt a shiver rack her body. A cold change was coming. In the five minutes she had been dithering outside, the sky had gone from clear to grey and a chill breeze now whipped about her. It would rain within a Melbourne minute.

The front door opened from the inside. A young woman was pushing it open with her bottom as she dragged a pram over the threshold behind her. Kelly leapt to grab the door to give her a hand.

The woman looked up, and her face broke into a beaming smile. 'Thanks!'

'No problem.'

Only once Kelly had watched the woman bounce the pram lightly down the steps did she realise she was still holding the door open. And it seemed wasteful to go through the whole intercom rigmarole when the main objective had already been achieved. She stepped inside and let the door swing shut behind her.

The foyer was spacious and elegant. Her high-heeled boots clack-clacked on the smooth marble floor. One solitary lift faced her. She pressed the up button, the down must have been for a hidden parking garage, very luxurious indeed in a city where all-day street parking was scarce.

The lift opened, she stepped inside and felt her last chance to run for her life slip away as the doors closed before her.

The mirrored walls reflected back a slim young woman of average height, shivering slightly in a slinky black barely-there halter-neck dress and knee-high black boots. Her long, thick dark hair, with month-old blonde streaks, was slicked back in a low ponytail, the wayward wisps of a growing-out fringe had been caught by the wind and now rested on her cheeks. Big sad brown eyes, her most striking feature, were rimmed in dark liner and lashings of mascara making them that much more dramatic.

The last time she had seen Simon she'd had short spiky hair, which she had chopped herself during her rebellious teens. She had been about a stone heavier, with enviable curves. She'd called it puppy-fat; he'd called her adorable. But living away from home, paying her own rent, with only sporadic pay cheques, had meant that certain luxuries, such as dinner, had been missed on the odd occasion. The puppy-fat had long since gone and she looked thin. Would he think too thin?

Who cares? she thought, standing up straighter, puffing out what little remained of her once ample chest. The reason she was there was to tell him that *whatever* he thought he should damn well keep it to himself.

The lift binged, and Kelly's heart slammed against her ribs. Her image wavered and split apart to reveal a small private foyer with a carved white door. It was ajar and Kelly could hear kitchen noises from inside. She sucked in a deep ragged breath, tucked her hair behind her ears, and walked in as if she owned the place.

It was beautiful. Polished wood floors led onto thick cream carpet, modern furniture, soft leather couches. Very opulent and worth a fortune. It was a place in which her parents would feel more than comfortable, so on the flipside it made her feel completely out of place. She was worried about leaving dirty tread on the carpet and wondered for a moment if she should have left her boots at the door.

A homely woman with grey hair tucked into an old-fashioned maid's cap poked her head around a doorway. 'Hello there.'

'Hello,' Kelly said back, hoping her facial features

were forming a confident smile and not the odd grimace she imagined. 'Is...Simon home?'

'Nope, sorry. Friend of Mr Coleman's, are you?'

A friend? Hardly. And it must be Simon's place—the cleaner had not said 'Simon who?' The woman watched Kelly carefully, and the broom in her hand seemed a ready weapon.

'Actually, I am his wife.' It felt odd, saying it out loud, but it was the only way she could think to avoid the humiliation of having to dodge a projectile broom handle as the woman became more suspicious by the second.

The woman raised her eyebrows in disbelief. 'I've heard nothing about a wife.'

'We have been...estranged.'

The woman nodded in sudden and all-too-ready understanding. 'That explains it. But now you are back. Glad to hear it. This place could do with a woman's touch. You wouldn't think Mr Coleman eats in; the kitchen is always so perfect. Make him a good meal. He needs one.'

Kelly nodded, though she had to suppress a smile. Her version of a home-cooked meal would be two-minute noodles.

The cleaner grabbed up her bits and bobs and headed for the front door. 'He should be home soon enough. Do lock up after if you're off first.' And she left, closing the door behind her with a soft click.

Kelly couldn't believe her luck, having time to case the joint, to get her bearings, to familiarise herself with all exits.

She walked about the apartment, trying to find signs of the boy who had stolen her heart when she was eleven years old, the teenager who had shared her first magical kiss at fourteen, and the young man who had married her in a secret ceremony on St Kilda beach at midnight on her eighteenth birthday.

No photographs lined the walls or side tables. No ornaments or collectibles showed signs of travel. There was simply no sign of the Simon Coleman she knew. Nothing of the sculptor, nothing of the sailor, nothing of the free spirit. She suddenly felt wary that this was not him. This guy with the cool, personality-free apartment could not be her Simon.

Hearing the jingle of keys at the front door, she spun on her heels. The world turned in agonising slow motion. The door banged lightly and the handle jiggled. Finally it opened and she stole a head-to-toe glance at the owner of the apartment: Simon of St Kilda.

And without a hint of a doubt Kelly knew she looked upon her husband.

CHAPTER TWO

KELLYISM:
LOVE SAYS LISTEN TO YOUR HEART?
'SINGLE AND LOVING IT!' SAYS LISTEN TO YOUR STOMACH.
THAT AIN'T BUTTERFLIES, THAT'S PURE ADRENALIN,
AND IT'S TELLING YOU TO RUN FOR YOUR LIFE!

SURE it was Simon, but if Kelly thought she had changed he was a revelation in evolution.

Caught in one of those surprising Melbourne rain showers, Simon was drenched from head to toe. He was slick with rainwater, his wet dark hair had been raked back by his fingers, and his jet-black T-shirt clung to every muscular curve of his chest. This was the lanky guy she had married five years before? This was a god!

Along with the new classic short back-and-sides haircut, his face had changed. The newly flat planes of his smooth cheeks book-ended his lovely straight nose and revealed the most glorious cheekbones Kelly had never guessed were hidden there. The delicious hazel eyes below his furrowed brow were still deep enough to drown in, though they too were changed. Where they had once been so very kind they were now cool, closed, guarded.

But if all else had altered, the mouth would have clinched it for her. That mouth would have reeled her in all on its own. The natural curve was just so kissable and the corners were for ever turned with the hint of a

16

private smile. Added to that those lips were now sleek with fresh rainwater.

From deep down in places she had forgotten even existed, a concoction of sensations and emotions dragged themselves to the surface. Her reaction to him was out of practice but as it always had been. Inevitable. Knee-weakening. And blinding. She had always found him beautiful. Inside and out. So much so her heart raced so that she could hardly breathe. And he hadn't even yet looked her way.

Get a grip, Kelly. Cool. Think cool.

She swallowed down her clambering ardour, because now she knew how little these feelings meant in the grand scheme of things. In the course of writing *Single and Loving It!* she had talked to dozens of other women who had been in similar boats, and had changed her view dramatically.

Her feelings for him had been understandable teenage lust and now she was just experiencing an echo of those sensations. Like her belly ring, her chopped hair and her hippy aspirations, it had been the perfect rebellion against her conservative parents. It had never really been love in the first place. Relentless passion, and unceasing adoration, sure. But love? That she now very much doubted.

'Hello, Simon.'

His head snapped up, his eyes narrowed. A moment later they softened, lit from within, their hazel depths flickering with warm gold, and beneath the altered exterior her Simon gazed back at her. And she all but melted.

'Hello, Kelly.'

His smooth, low voice washed over her like a warm

sun shower. The five years since she had heard him speak slipped away and it felt as if it had been no more than five minutes.

'I assume you got my letter,' he said and Kelly remembered why she was there and she was much obliged as the gulf between them widened once more.

This was no happy reunion with her long-lost best friend. This was no time to fall into a hopeless, trembling puddle at her former lover's feet. This was an intervention.

The day she signed a freelance contract doing the perfect, made-for-her job, writing about how to live without a man, her husband turned up on the scene. He was a thorn in the side of the wonderful new life she had created for herself and he had to be removed, fast, before he became too deeply imbedded.

'I did get your preposterous letter,' she said, 'and I would appreciate it if that was the last of its kind.'

'Fine. Don't write rubbish and I will have no reason to refute it.'

Her first response was a slow, steadying blink as he walked past her without another glance and took his bags of groceries into the kitchen. She followed, striving to drag her treacherous gaze from the tempting sight of tanned, tensed forearm muscles as he carried the heavy load.

'Rubbish?' she yelled when she finally found her voice. 'I would have you know the women I write about are all real people. Real women with real experiences and real hopes that have been dashed one too many times by *men*.' She all but spat the word in his face.

He continued to unpack his groceries all but ignoring her outburst. 'That column of yours has to be damaging.

Individual women have the capacity to make up their own minds about their individual relationships. The last thing they need is some unqualified post-feminist hack spreading easy wholesale answers to serious situations.'

Kelly coughed and spluttered her way back into the conversation. 'I would have you know that it is the most popular new column in the magazine's history.'

He shrugged. 'Popularity is fleeting and not something to hang your hat on. Think plaid flares. Think fluorescent socks. Need I go on?'

'Readers love me!'

'I thought your job was to convince your readers there was no such thing as love.'

She counted to ten in her mind. 'No such thing as romantic, everlasting love between a man and a woman. Respect and heartfelt thanks are out there in droves and they are coming my way.'

'Fine. You are a star. But you are also a liar.'

Steam was streaming from her ears, literally, she was certain. She could feel it heating up her scalp! 'Me? A liar? How dare you—?'

The steam faded. She *was* a liar, wasn't she? Of sorts. Nobody knew she was married. But then again she did not know if Maya was married. And to all intents and purposes she was alone. And single. But before she could tell Simon just how wrong he was, he turned on her.

'Did you actually read my letter?'

Only a hundred times. 'Yes,' she said through clenched teeth.

'And that's why you're here?'

'Of course. Nothing else would possibly have dragged

me here. But my editor wants me to respond to your ridiculous statements in the next column.'

Simon smiled, his beautiful mouth turning up at the sides and revealing lovely, naturally neat white teeth. Her heart leapt. She mentally slapped it down.

'Good,' he said. 'I look forward to hearing your response.'

'My response, Simon, is that you can stick your letter up your—'

Simon's sensibilities were saved by the shrill ringing of his mobile phone. He turned away and answered it. His voice switched into professional mode. After a few moments he put his hand over the mouthpiece and said, 'It's my broker. Won't be a moment. Don't go away.' He walked out of the room, talking residuals and percentages as he went.

She had never seen him talk like that to anyone. Her Simon had been a thinker, a dreamer, not someone who lived in a museum, carried the latest in mobile phones, and had a stockbroker! And not someone who could demand her to stay with such authority that she could not help but shoot him a saucy salute behind his departing back.

After a few moments she followed, intrigued despite herself, and peeked around the corner.

He was in his bedroom and it was as sparse and flavourless as the rest of the apartment. He had already whipped off his soaked top and tossed it on a gargantuan white bed and was pulling the belt from his trousers. One glance at the broad naked shoulders and tanned buff chest on show was enough for Kelly to spring back into the dining room, her heart beating a million miles a minute and her head swimming with mixed images of Simon at twenty-one, slim and fit, to be sure, but certainly not the strapping man she had just glimpsed.

Well, several seconds of solid ogling were probably more than a glimpse…

Kelly's self-consciousness returned in full measure. She worried that compared to her eighteen-year-old self she looked too thin, too grown up. She rushed through the bare apartment searching frantically for a mirror and had to settle for her reflection in the microwave.

She needed all the body armour she could muster. She tugged at her dress, smoothed out her hair, ran a finger under each eye to make sure her eyeliner was even. She sucked in her stomach, puffed out her minimal chest and waited for her one-time paramour to return.

He did, soon enough, wearing dry chocolate-brown trousers and a deep red shirt, untucked with the top two buttons open showing a glimpse of the enviable physique beneath, and went straight to unpacking his groceries without even a glance her way.

Even in her barely-there dress she felt hot. Hot and bothered. Yet he had barely even taken in her sexy short dress. She had not caught him checking out her legs or anything! It was plainly obvious he was not back for all that and she fought to squash the rising disappointment. So why was he back?

'Why are you writing this column, Kelly?'

'To pay the rent,' she spat out. It meant infinitely more to her than that but she had no intention of letting him know the power he held by simply being on the scene.

His hands stopped shuffling for a brief moment before taking up where they left off.

'With folks like yours I wouldn't have thought that would be a major concern for you.' He must have sensed the scream welling inside her as he continued. 'Or why not stick to obituaries?'

That stifled the scream in an instant. So he had been keeping up with her career for a while. It had been months since she'd had the reward of that particular job.

'Why write *this* column?'

'Because I have the *in-the-trenches* experience to have real insight. With *Single and Loving It!* I really have something valuable to say.'

'Which is?'

'Love is an illusion and what the illusion promises exists in the woman's mind alone and *never* in real life.'

She wondered if he too felt the words sounded rehearsed, as though she had repeated them like a mantra inside her head a thousand times before.

His glance shifted her way and held and all the body armour in the world could not have kept her safe. Kelly's breath faltered. Her skin warmed. And her long-since-dormant libido whirred back to life. As, standing before her, his beautiful hazel eyes boring into hers, he seemed as far from an illusion as could be.

'Do you really believe that?' he finally asked.

Kelly swallowed. How was a woman to stand up to *such* focussed attention from *such* a man? Unless armed with the knowledge that the promise in his eyes and the tumbling feelings in her own stomach were all precursors to disillusionment, any woman would be sucked in only to be spat out at a later date. Thankfully her column was around to prepare women for just such an occasion.

'I do believe it,' she said, and she meant it.

Simon shook his head and several damp locks of hair flicked onto his forehead and it was all Kelly could do not to close the distance between them, reach out, and brush them away, just as she would have done all those years before. How could she expect her readers to follow her advice to disregard the very real physical sensations one experienced at times like this if she was finding it so hard?

All the more reason to be strong.

'Why are you here?' she asked.

'This is my apartment.'

Kelly's fingernails dug into her palms. 'I mean why are you back? In Melbourne?' *Living barely streets away from me?*

Simon turned back to his groceries and Kelly expelled the breath she had been holding. He loaded up a platter with fresh bread sticks, soft cheeses, and other trimmings and walked into the dining room. Kelly could do little but follow. He set the platter down, and pulled out a chair for her. When she remained standing, he pressed her into the seat, his achingly familiar fingers leaving warm imprints on her bare shoulders, then sat in a chair on the other side of the gleaming oval table.

'I am back for all sorts of reasons.'

'Being?' she prompted. Not fair for him to grill her and expect to be let off the hook.

'Work. Family.'

If you took that to the nth degree she would be considered family.

'How are your family?' she asked, deciding to take his statement literally.

'Well, actually.' He softened immeasurably, his secret smile once more tugging at the corner of his mouth. 'My sister is married with two kids now.'

'Nikki or Kat?' Wow. Neither was even dating when she had last seen them.

'Nikki. Kat is a nanny in London.'

'And your mother?' Kelly knew this had always been a sore point for Simon but she had to ask. She had always truly liked Simon's mother despite her shortfalls.

'She's good. Really good. Remarried and living in Sydney.'

Again? Kelly thought, wondering if that would be the fourth marriage or if she had married more times since their estrangement.

Simon grabbed a hunk of bread, lathered it in a hefty chunk of Brie and a good measure of pepper before popping it on a plate and handing it to Kelly. She stared at the food. She had not eaten this exact combination since the night of their wedding. Had he remembered or was it a fluke?

She glanced up and saw him making his own favourite with Swiss cheese and cherry tomatoes. This felt all too intimate. All too familiar. All too far from where she had imagined she would be when she'd woken up that morning.

But her poor neglected stomach rumbled in anticipation of the delicious-looking food so she bit down. It was as delicious as she remembered but the bread soon stuck in her throat as the memories that it invoked came tumbling down upon her. She placed the remaining food on the plate and wiped the telltale crumbs from her fingers.

'How long have you been back, Simon?'

'A little over a week.'

Her heart wrenched. It had taken him that long to contact her, and even then it had been in a most obscure manner. Despite her promises to be strong it ached to think they had once been the best of friends and here they were engaging in small talk like a pair of acquaintances.

He made no apology and did not seem even to notice the awkwardness of the situation.

'It was a couple of weeks ago,' he continued, 'when I overheard several women in my office talking about this amazing new column called *Single and Loving It!*. Because of the column they had decided to cancel their plans to go to a nightclub that weekend and were instead going to have a few girlfriends around for a night at home.'

Kelly listened in silence to the familiar story, concentrating on his expression as he retold the tale. And where usually people would have a glimmer in their eye, as if they were sharing in some grand inside joke about the perils of singlehood, Simon watched her with a shuttered expression, all evidence of good humour gone.

'I was about to move on until one of them said, "That Kelly Rockford is my new hero. She's a genius. I wish she had been writing this column five years ago. Would have saved me a lot of wasted Saturday nights." Understandably that caught my attention.'

The corner of his mouth kicked, revealing a sexy crease in his right cheek. *You cannot keep a good smile down,* Kelly thought, feeling her stomach warm absurdly in response.

'I asked around, found *Fresh*, and saw not genius but sadness. I saw not the wit and vivacity of the Kelly Rockford I had once known but hostility and bitterness that I refused to believe could come from the same woman. Even when your picture appeared above your byline, I had to come and see for myself in order to believe it was really you.'

He stopped talking and looked her over. Kelly straightened up under the meticulous inspection.

'You've changed, Kell.'

The shortening of her name flowed over her like the endearment it once had been. She shook it off.

'Not surprising,' she scoffed, 'considering it *has* been five years.'

'Still…' His voice trailed off.

Still what? she ached to ask. *Still you expected me to be the bubbly bundle of fun and fancy I was at eighteen. Well, you're the one who eradicated that girl, my friend.*

'Am I to take it that after five years of nothing, after five years of not having the courtesy to let me know if you were dead or alive, you are only *now* back simply to assure yourself that I have not become all bitter and twisted?'

After five years of my not knowing if you were healthy and happy. If you had moved on to other relationships. Or if you still missed me so much it physically hurt.

His mouth opened. He had something to say, Kelly was sure of it. She waited in agonising anticipation for answers to questions that had plagued her for years. But he must have thought better of it and clammed his mouth shut. And that was enough for Kelly to regain her purpose. She gathered up every last ounce of courage and laid it on the line.

'Well, for whatever reason you are here, you are here. And we have managed to avoid talking about this since we haven't, well, *talked* in the last five years. But this is just ridiculous. We really can't go on being married.'

His warm eyes glossed over so fast, so icy cold, it made her shiver. 'Is there someone else you wish to be married to?' he asked. He took a slow bite of his bread but his gaze held fast to hers.

'No!' Kelly shook her head manically and flapped her hands in front of her face.

Simon's smile warmed up again, this time even enough to showcase a sexy crease on *each* cheek and she cringed.

Hmm. Probably could have made that 'no' less emphatic.

'So what's the rush?' he asked, his expression a model of nonchalance.

If my readers find out I am married, my life as I know it is all over! That's the rush!

'Five years is hardly a rush. And considering I could not find you for the first three, that shortens the time span a little.'

The last of the cool in his eyes melted. 'You looked for me?'

'What do you think I did? Do you think I just said, "Oh, well, my husband has disappeared, but them's the breaks, so may as well get on with the rest of my life"?'

Still he was silent, yet he seemed to be basking in the knowledge that she had cared enough to search. And it made Kelly furious. The hurt, the confusion, and the loss she had spent five years overcoming swarmed in on her all over again.

'Well, think again, boyo. You may have enjoyed running off to the other side of the country and reinventing yourself into this!' She flicked a hand around the cool apartment. 'But I was left here to face my family and try to explain why the man I had spent my life defending had done the very thing they had always warned me he would do.'

The warmth in Simon's eyes switched to a burning flame. 'I bet they relished the fact.'

Kelly jumped to her feet and slammed her hands on the table.

'Of course they did! You proved them right. What about proving me right? What about proving yourself right?'

'I think I have done that, don't you?'

'No. Unless all this is some sort of charade, you have sold out. But somehow I don't think it is. I would put money on the fact you would have more suits in your closet than old jeans, and if so you have become what they wanted you to be. Not what I loved you for being.' Her voice finally cracked. The cool Kelly act was fast coming apart at the seams.

Simon slid to his feet and was around her side of the table in a second. His hands taking a tight hold on her upper arms were the only things keeping her upright.

She wished he would stop looking at her like that. As if he was so sure he was right. As if he had all the answers and all she had to do was surrender to them. His beautiful hazel eyes burned deep into her mind.

'I have become what *you* always knew I would be, Kelly. I am wealthy. I am successful. Just as you always predicted.'

And then she realised he was only centimetres away. Not the miles and miles he had been for so very long. Centimetres could so easily become millimetres and then she would be enfolded in his strong arms. But she knew, from his fervid objection to what she had become, if he even sensed what she was feeling he would be appalled by the very thought.

It is all just an echo, she reminded herself, *an echo*

of bygone desire. A mirage, a shimmering memory that belongs where it came from. In the past. He is here to ease his own guilt, no other reason.

Kelly's strength returned and she pulled away, rubbing away the tingle in her arms where he had held her. Her head swam. She had to get away. Away from the stifling apartment. Away from him.

'No, Simon, you are wrong. What I wanted was for you to do whatever you felt you had to do, but with me at your side. But that is all water under the bridge now. Now I want a divorce. I'll send you the papers.'

She turned and walked to the front door, her legs all but turning to jelly beneath her. As she closed the door she looked his way one more time and her heart lurched in her chest as she watched him slump into the dining-room chair and lower his head into his hands.

Kelly felt more herself when her home, St Kilda Storeys, an old, no-frills apartment building located a block from the beach, came into view. Her parents thought it a run-down hovel but Kelly preferred to think it had loads of character. Add to that the fantastic location, and the dozen fabulous young neighbours, on her meagre budget she could not have hoped for better.

When Kelly opened her top-floor apartment door her tiny dog, Minky, bounded into her waiting arms.

'Hey, baby doll,' Kelly cooed. 'Gracie not home?' she asked the diddering dog.

Kelly called out, but her flatmate must have left already. She worked shifts at the Crown Casino as a croupier in the high rollers room so they crossed paths between shifts and on weekends, which worked well for both and gave Minky plenty of company.

But right then Kelly wished her little-seen flatmate were home. She needed a friendly ear. She kept Minky with her and walked back down the stairs until she reached the ground-floor apartment.

She knocked on the door. Her other Saturday Night Cocktails buddy, the young owner of the St Kilda Storeys apartment block, and sometime stylist for *Fresh*, classy Cara, opened up chewing on a slice of honey-covered toast. Kelly eyed the food and salivated. Minky did the same.

Cara happily fed them both. And when she heard the good news, she threw her arms around Kelly, careful to keep her sticky, crumby fingers away from her friend. 'A contracted columnist at *Fresh*. Didn't I tell you the two of you were made for each other?'

'So I can get you the rent in a week if you can wait.'

Cara fluffed a hand across her face. 'Next week's fine. Don't worry about it. So *Single and Loving It!* is here to stay. But can you do it? Is there enough vitriol in that tiny frame of yours to castigate men infinitum?'

Kelly thought back to Simon's self-righteous certainty and nodded. 'You bet. With more and more ammunition coming my way on a daily basis.'

'Ooh, that sounds juicy. What happened?'

'Ran into an ex today.' Close enough. 'Wasn't fun. But did make me feel that much more right about sending my ideas and resolutions out into the world for other women to emulate.'

'How not fun? Details, darlin'.'

How was it not fun? They had been fairly polite. They had even broken bread together. It had all been terribly civilised. And that was where the fun was lost. In the past they had been beyond passionate. Whether clawing at each other's throats or at each other's clothes, the one thing they had never been was civilised.

'Saving it for the column.'

'Thank God names must be changed to protect the innocent or I have a feeling this guy would be pulp by the time you were finished with him.'

And Kelly smiled. Simon had blown that one. By writing to her and begging a response, there would be no need for protecting the innocent. Or the guilty as the case might be.

'Cocktails Saturday night?' Cara asked.

'Always,' Kelly promised, planting a kiss on her friend's cheek. 'Thanks for the ear, Cara. I'd better go.'

Kelly had a column to map out and the ideas were flowing thick and fast.

CHAPTER THREE

KELLYISM:
YEARNING FOR A MAN WITH WHOM TO SPEND YOUR TIME? GET A HOBBY INSTEAD!

BY SIX the next morning Kelly was up at the front of her kickboxing class. She had almost become used to picturing her mother's disappointed face on the punching bag and to have Simon's face there in its place felt like a huge step backwards.

But it was enough to put extra vigour into her kick. She spun on her left heel and her right foot caught the huge bag precisely in the centre, sending a satisfying zing up her leg.

The capability to kick the sense out of a perfectly docile leather bag had been her saviour and a much more affordable option than the therapy her mother had offered to pay for. Twice a week for five years had kept her fit and kept her mind clear. You couldn't mope and achieve the addictive endorphin rush at the same time, so she'd had to give up one for the other.

Kelly jogged on the spot, working up a sweat and a new appetite to take on Simon's assertions head-on. The more ammunition she had, the better her column would be. She had found at least one wonderful woman to feature this week, and she knew that Simon's insensitivity to the delicate nature of a woman's heart would be obvious in comparison.

Kelly slowed to a light bounce. Class was over. But a few last-minute punches to a point on the bag about six feet off the ground did not go astray.

Kelly hopped off the tram and walked the block to the melon-coloured two-storey stuccoed building that held the offices of *Fresh* magazine. It was her first full day as a real staff writer at *Fresh*.

The world was a good place. One or two minor irritations could be brushed over as long as she had the job of her dreams, a forum from which she could spread the word. *Be fearless. Be resolute. Be heard. And whatever else, be who you have to be.*

She pushed open the glass doors that led to the front reception and all but gasped as she saw Simon leaning on the reception desk.

It was bad enough having to face him in his apartment when she'd had time to prepare herself, but him showing up in her place of work shocked the hell out of her. Besides, he was dressed down in a form-fitting white T-shirt, jeans and cowboy boots, and he looked unbelievable. It was too much to cope with all at once.

Upon Kelly's arrival, Judy, the receptionist, stopped batting her eyelashes at Simon at once, leapt from her swivel chair and disappeared into the office behind her.

'What are you doing here?' Kelly snapped, her eyes darting about the open space to see if anyone was within hearing distance. 'Apart from flirting with my co-workers, that is?'

Simon's eyes narrowed and Kelly wished she had learnt the ability to keep her trap shut. She was learning that telling it as it was in print was one thing, but thinking before speaking could not be overrated.

'We had not finished our conversation when you ran off yesterday,' Simon said.

'I did not run off. I left. Something you should recognise since you are such an expert at it.'

He didn't even blanch. Pity. Standing there before her all manly and gorgeous, with all that healthy glowing tan, was entirely too disconcerting.

'Besides, I had said all I wished to say to you.' Kelly tilted her nose in the air and walked past Simon on stiff legs. 'Now please leave. Anything else you have to say can be said through a lawyer.'

Simon shot out a hand and took Kelly by the arm. His hand was warm beneath the steely strength, and it felt so deliciously familiar. *Familiar.* She looked down at his hand. It was large and square, with clean clipped fingernails. But it was not soft like that of a man who worked in an office all day. It was lightly roughened from outdoor work as it always had been. So, beneath the city-worker exterior there were hints of the Simon who had lived his life in the sunshine, who did not stop working on his beloved boats until the weak moonlight made it impossible.

'You really have changed,' he said, all but mirroring Kelly's thoughts.

She shot him her steeliest glare. 'You said that already.'

'It's just that it hits me anew each time I see you.'

His coarse grip softened but did not let go. He ran his unfathomable hazel eyes over her, taking in every inch of her that was so different. And she was glad she had made a concerted effort that morning.

Her hair was ironed straight and hanging sleekly past her shoulder blades. But as his gaze raked over it, long where it had once been pixie-short, she could almost feel his craving to reach out and stroke its silky length and she fought the urge to rake it back into an unexciting ponytail.

Her lashes were lathered in their usual black mascara, her cheeks were dusted in a shimmering pink, and her lips were awash with pale rose gloss. Her tight black top was held together with a small clip at her belly and fanned out again to reach the top of her skirt, showcasing décolletage, what cleavage she could muster, and belly, which were flushed with bronzing powder. Her skirt, which was black and pencil-thin, stopped just below her knees and she wore pointy black stilettos.

It was the outfit of a magazine chick, a woman with great self-assurance, and no fear. An outfit Kelly had chosen to get her through the most important day of her life so far. An outfit she had not seen as daring when wearing it in offices staffed mainly by women in similar garb, but standing there under Simon's unashamed scrutiny she felt half naked.

'I can't get over how different you look.'

Kelly knew it too. She looked worn-down, thin.

His gaze finally raked back to hers and her breath caught painfully in her throat as she waited for him to say so.

The enchanting creases slowly, slowly, deepened in his smooth cheeks as an intimate smile lit his handsome face and he said, 'You are beautiful, Kell.'

She blinked to cover her shock. He had never called her beautiful before. Cute. Adorable. Sexy. But never, *ever* beautiful.

Only then did she realise with utter astonishment that it was not disappointment or guilt resting heavily in his piercing hazel eyes, but desire. And in complete disregard for the consequences she felt herself leaning into his magnetic pull, being drawn deeper and deeper into his beautiful, longing gaze. Her breath released on a deep sigh and its message was loud and clear. The libido that had reawakened only the day before was up and running full steam ahead. She was turned on beyond measure.

'Kelly?'

She blinked, rocked back onto her stiletto heels, and turned to the dismembered voice. Maya was standing in the open doorway to the offices, with Judy hovering behind her. Maya looked curiously from Kelly to the man seated nonchalantly on the desk at her side with one hand wrapped possessively around her arm.

'What are you up to all the way out here, my sweet?'

Simon released his grip and stood, and Kelly knew he was moving to introduce himself. And the last thing she needed was to be shown up as a fraud on her first real day at work. Her world clicked back into focus.

'This is Simon,' Kelly shouted, drawing all eyes her way. 'Simon of St Kilda. He is here to be interviewed for my next column.'

Maya's eyes opened wide in surprise. 'Well, well, Ms Rockford. You are a revelation. How on earth did you find this fellow and so quickly?'

Yes, how? How? How on earth? Anything but the facts. Her frantic mind tumbled over the possibilities and came up with…nothing.

'A woman should never reveal her sources, her secrets, nor her deepest desires,' Simon filled in the deep silence. 'Wasn't that a *Kellyism* from a couple of weeks back?'

Maya nodded, impressed. 'I see you are a true connoisseur of our Kelly's column.'

'I have read it with great personal interest.'

'Glad to hear it. I will leave you two to it. Bleed him dry, Kelly. I have a feeling about this one.'

Maya winked at Simon and left in a sparkling silver wake and a wash of expensive perfume, with a madly blushing Judy hot on her heels.

Kelly had gathered her wits and purposely funnelled her tension into sharp anger. She pointed to the front door. 'Now go!'

'Can't. I'm being interviewed by a hot new writer.'

Simon sunk his hands into his jeans pockets, whistled a merry tune, and walked around Kelly and into the offices. She was left alone, pointing to the front door, feeling certain the emphasis on *hot* was not accidental.

When she caught up with Simon he was wandering through the open-plan room, the eyes of every woman in the place overtly following him. He received a few inviting smiles, a couple of assertive hellos, and even a wolf-whistle from the graphics department.

He turned to Kelly. 'Which one's yours?'

She pointed to her tiny desk and suddenly wished she had not made herself so at home so soon. Simon took a seat and pored over the photos stuck to her monitor.

Photos of her last birthday party, with her sitting at the old wooden table in her apartment, surrounded by Cara, Gracie, and other tenants, with sponge cake and cream all over her face. Photos of her cuddling Minky on her *single* bed. And a more staid photo of her last Christmas, sitting on her parents' huge leather couch by a ridiculously large tree decorated in elegant silver ornaments. Kelly nibbled on her thumbnail and watched as Simon caught up on her life over the past five years.

Simon looked beyond the family shot and grabbed the one of Minky. 'Is she...how is she?'

'Scruffy and spoilt as ever.'

'Missing me?'

'Not any more.'

He did not glance her way though she was sure he had got her message loud and clear.

'And your parents?'

'Painful and…painful as ever.'

'Missing me?' He looked up with this question, his expression playful.

This brought a curious smile to Kelly's face. 'More than life itself.'

The smile stayed. Five years before, any mention of her parents would have started a fight. They had warned her from the start that he would be like his mother and flee at the first sign of hard work in a relationship and he had never forgiven them for it. And when he had left they had lived for months on 'I told you so'.

But now here was a Simon who could ask after her parents with a smile on his face, in self-deprecation. Wonder of wonders.

As he put the picture back he bumped the mouse and stared as Kelly's monitor changed from a star field screensaver to the shot of a crystal-clear ocean with a beautiful white sailing boat bobbing imperiously atop it.

It was the brochure shot of their boat. The one they had spent their brief passionate wedding night aboard. She rushed to her desk and clicked open a Word file, the blank white page obliterating the offending picture.

'So, where do you want to start?' Kelly asked.

Simon dragged his eyes from the computer screen, his look filled with questions Kelly did not dare answer, even to herself.

'You said you were here to be interviewed so we may as well go through with it.' Kelly made herself busy fluffing about in her filing cabinet until she found the letter. It was crumpled from a moment of wrath when she had rolled it into the smallest ball she could, stomped on it until flat, then shoved it at the very bottom of her rubbish bin. Eventually reason had made her iron it out with her hands but it still looked worse for wear. She could feel Simon's smile as he saw the paper.

'I was picturing your face as I did it,' Kelly said quietly, knowing there were a dozen pairs of ears trained onto their cubicle.

'I figured as much. So what would you like to ask me?'

Kelly leaned against the cubicle wall, arms folded, as Simon twisted and bounced on her chair. There was no way out of it now. Maya had seen him. She would have to grab a couple of lines for the column to take the edge off Maya's curiosity.

'Okay, then. Why do you think you know any more than I do about...?'

'Love?' he finished for her in a voice so low and reminiscent of the nights he would whisper such words in her ear by bonfires on the beach.

'Mmm.' She could not bring herself to say the word.

'I don't claim to know any more than you do. I think I know about exactly the same amount.'

'Ha!' She scoffed so loud a couple of female heads turned her way, their eyes alight with interest.

'You disagree?' he asked.

'I'm the one asking the questions here,' she said through clenched teeth, her glance darting about the room.

'I have a question for you,' he said, happily ignoring her protest. 'Where's your ring?'

He reached out and took her left hand, toying with

her bare ring finger, encircling, stroking, caressing from the tip to her sensitive palm.

Kelly's gaze rocked back to him, startled. She knew which ring he meant. She yanked her hand away and rubbed at the spot that tingled with the memory of wearing the ring Simon had given her. Such a short time. Such a long time ago.

She shrugged. 'I haven't worn it in years. And I've moved so many times since then…who knows? Gone for all eternity, I suppose.'

He leaned back in the chair and crossed his arms. His gaze had lowered to her squirming hands so she had no idea how her answer affected him. But it had affected her to her very core. It had dredged up memories and feelings and associations with another time when he had held her left hand with such intimacy.

'So if you're the one asking the questions,' he finally said, 'come on, then. Ask away.'

Her mind froze. The only other question she could summon at that moment was: *Do you feel the same overwhelming and downright frightening sense of sense slipping away that I feel every time we are within touching distance of one another?*

So, knowing that was the last thing she wanted to share with Simon, she stood and grabbed him by the hand, dragging him through the room, past a dozen interested onlookers, and into the tearoom, which thankfully was empty.

'I don't think this is going to work. I have your letter. That's enough for me to come up with a perfectly good retort.'

'Surely I deserve a heads up. I said in my letter that I believe love is alive and well out there. What do you have to say about that?'

She still held his hand. She made to pull away and his free hand put a stop to that, closing over hers so that it was entirely encased in the strong warmth of his grasp.

Kelly was sure she had plenty to say but at that moment her throat had closed over and her pulse had quickened to a rate of knots. She shook her head to clear the indefinable fog that was dampening her perfectly good rage.

'Simon, just go, please.' Her voice sounded far away.

'No.'

'No?'

'No. I did not come here to be interviewed, Kelly, you know that.'

'So why are you here?'

Please tell me. Whatever the answer, I have to know.

He closed the gap between them so quickly Kelly did not see it coming. His warm, strong hands pulled her to him before reaching up, framing her shocked face as he leaned in to touch his lips to hers.

For a moment Kelly was able to resist. Stunned as she was. But only a moment. Then, with a shuddering groan, her open mouth yielded under his warm, persuasive skill.

Simon's beautiful lips tempted her own apart and a hundred distant memories burst to the surface with the unexpectedness of a lightning flash. She could all but feel the hot sun of five years before burn upon her neck as his kiss deepened and enticed and sent melting hot flushes the length of her body.

She stole her hands around his shoulders to bury her fingers deep into his soft hair, the silky sensation so familiar and so missed all these years. One of Simon's hands followed suit, sliding around to bury itself deep within her tumble of silky hair just as she had sensed him longing to do all morning. His other hand stole around her back, the heat from his fingertips scorching through the thin synthetic fabric of her top. It curved lower, and lower until he cupped her bottom.

Then, having wrapped her up tight in his solid embrace, Simon pressed his body to hers. He was muscled where he had once been lean. And even with the changes to her own physique he fitted as if he had been carved just for her.

And the one blaring thought that managed to seep through her whirling, foggy, out-of-control mind was that she ached to know every single one of those changes up close and personal.

CHAPTER FOUR

KELLYISM:
LOVE AND KISSES SHOULD NEVER BE USED
IN THE SAME SENTENCE,
UNLESS IT'S THIS ONE!

KELLY'S mobile phone buzzed at her hip. The vibration jolted her out of Simon's arms as if she had been struck with a hot poker.

She pulled away, relieved beyond thought that nobody had walked in on them. That was all she needed: to be caught necking in the tearoom. How could she, the mentor of how to survive without a man, explain *that* to her new colleagues?

She reached for the phone and checked the text message, blissfully ignoring Simon who was standing in front of her, his hands hanging clenched at his sides, his chest rising and falling with the same power and pace as her own.

'My *real* interview is on the phone,' Kelly said. She looked to him with pleading eyes. 'So stay, go, do whatever you please, just leave me alone.'

'I'll go. For now.'

For ever. Please, for my sanity's sake, go for ever this time.

He left and she followed. And as he reached the doorway to Reception, he sent her one last glance. One last hot, meaningful, and totally knee-weakening glance. It

43

was all she could do to send him a professional nod and walk calmly back towards her desk. She could feel dozens of pairs of eyes burning holes into her back.

She'd kissed him. What on earth was she thinking kissing him? Sure, he had started it but that was an excuse better suited to the school playground. And she had certainly joined in without hesitation. Argh! She had been trying to send him away, for good, and then she had gone and kissed him! *Well done, Kelly. Now he'll really take your demands to get lost seriously.*

She reached her desk and sat down with a punishing thud. A pretty blonde head popped around from the desk across from hers.

'Hiya.'

'Hello.'

'I'm Lena.' The cute girl extended a plump hand. 'I'm the restaurant critic. You're Kelly Rockford, right?'

'I am.' Kelly's breathing had thankfully slowed to a more regular pace. She shook the proffered hand.

'Glad to have you on board,' Lena said. '*Single and Loving It!* is a crack-up. My girlfriends and I are totally addicted. One friend broke up with her boyfriend last week and we actually did your ritual night, right down to burning her ex's photo and dancing around the ashes. Felt so silly at first but my friend is like I have never seen her. She is on top of the world. You saved her, and us from having to put up with the usual blubbering mess we would have had to contend with. You're a genius.'

Kelly smiled, picturing the night a week after Simon had left when she had performed that ritual herself. Naked on the beach at midnight. Burning every photograph, every piece of physical evidence that he had been a part of her life. Doing everything she could to release her downtrodden spirit and move on. Though she was only now realising the little good it had done in releasing her from his influence.

'Oh, no. Don't go thinking I am a genius. Just a medium through which women can be heard.'

'Believe me. I can't wait to see what you come up with next. Anyway, grab me if you have any questions about the place. Happy to help.'

'Thanks, Lena, shall do.'

Lena grinned at her as if she were a movie star and swung back inside her own cubicle.

Kelly took a deep breath and picked up her phone. 'Judy, could you patch my interviewee through for me? Thanks.'

Kelly sat at Maya's desk that afternoon as the elder woman glanced over her outline. Her face spread into a wide grin.

'This is priceless. Is she for real?'

Kelly nodded.

'Wherever do you find these women?' Before Kelly could answer Maya waved her quiet. 'Sorry, sorry, I forgot. ''A woman should never reveal her sources, her secrets, nor her deepest desires.'' The way that young Simon of St Kilda came out with that line made me want to have secrets just so he could come looking for them!'

'Maya!' Kelly could not control her blush at Maya's ravenous expression.

'He's a dish. No doubt about it.' After a brief sigh Maya continued as though there had been no pit stop in the conversation. 'So this Gillian woman crashes weddings on a regular basis.'

'Yep. Every weekend. Sometimes twice a week.'

'Whatever for?'

'It seems she just loves weddings. Loves the unadulterated joy experienced on such occasions that you find nowhere else.'

'Women are amazing creatures. Even I am shocked by what some of my sisters get up to in their private moments. How men have a chance in hell of figuring us out is beyond me.' Maya threw the pages onto the desk. 'I'll green light this story, no worries. So how are you going with the dish? Does *he* still think he has you figured out?'

'I certainly hope not,' Kelly said, feigning a confidence she did not feel.

'Did you get the dirt on him?

If only she knew!

'Not terribly forthcoming, unfortunately.'

'What is his story, I wonder? His background? By the heat in that letter he sent you there has to be a grand story to tell. Is he single? Is he married? Is he straight? Has he been burned? It's up to you to find out, my young friend. If an old dog like me is this wound up about him, imagine how our sweet young readers will react. They will be practically palpitating with wonder!'

Kelly nodded slowly, thanking her lucky stars it was up to her and not any of the other staffers. At least this way she could keep it all under wraps until he was gone again. Because he would go again. That was undeniable. It was in his genes. Until then Kelly would just have to juggle her writing, his appearances, and Maya's interest. Her nerves began to twinge as she watched Maya's interest expand before her eyes.

'Instead of writing up a separate response, can you work him into this article somehow?'

Kelly shook her head. 'I don't think so. I really don't think there is anything of interest there. And the wedding crasher is too good a hook to pass up.'

Maya clapped her hands together. 'I have had an epiphany.'

Kelly had the distinct feeling she was not going to like this particular epiphany one bit.

'This weekend you and the dish are going to get all gussied up and crash a wedding together.'

No! No!

'No!'

Maya raised a thin silver eyebrow.

'I mean it would be much easier if it was just me tagging along with Gillian. The more of us there are, the more likely we are to be caught.'

'So? Getting caught would have to be an even better story than not. So it's settled. Get in touch with your mystery fan and hook him up. He seemed like a guy who would give anything a go. I'm sure he won't disagree. And you can use the time there to dig for dirt. Get his angle. I want to know all there is to know about your guy.'

Maya bustled her out of the office and Kelly left feeling the weight of the world on her shoulders, but really it was only the weight of the tumble of deceptions she had wrapped herself in.

But Maya knew her stuff. If the truth came out about *her guy*, it would make for an astonishing story.

Kelly's mobile phone rang whilst she was in the tram on the way home from work.

'Darling!' her mother called from a cruise ship in the Pacific Ocean. 'I heard all about your promotion. That is wonderful!'

'Hi, Mum.' Kelly sighed. 'It's not actually a promotion. It's just more permanent.'

'Either way, your father and I are so proud of you.

We simply must do something special to celebrate once we get back on land. And now maybe you have your foot in the door you can write something…different. Something nicer.'

'Mum, my column is the reason I got the contract. It's really touched a nerve in the world of twenty-something single women.'

Kelly grimaced a smile at a twenty-something woman on the other side of the tram who was watching her with understanding. Girls and their mothers could fill a whole other column entirely. The girl smiled back and rolled her eyes.

'Yes, well, it's all a bit angry for my taste. Maybe if I could find you a nice young man down at the club you would find nicer things to write about. There is a new tennis instructor. He was on the pro tour for a couple of years.'

'Mum, I am still married, remember? Do you want me committing adultery?'

If there was one way to change the subject, that was it. Though Kelly did not for a moment consider telling her mother Simon was back in town. That would only cause panic and she would never get off the phone at that rate. Besides, Simon was her problem. And she had spent years making sure she did not need anybody else to fix her problems.

'At least now you can move out of that…place and into somewhere more appropriate. Your father is on the case already. Just before the trip he found a lovely spot in Hawthorn. Jill Maybury's daughters live there. It has twenty-four-hour security and a tennis court and is right around the corner from The House.'

As always Kelly was rankled by the way her mother said *The House* as if it deserved capital letters.

And her mother had no clue. With this job, it meant she could afford to pay the rent, buy groceries and maybe spoil herself once in a while by treating herself at one of the unbelievable French pastry shops on Acland Street. An apartment with security and a tennis court was a fair way off yet, unless Mum and Dad added to the coffers, which she had a feeling would be the next kindly offer. Thanks, but no, thanks.

'I love my apartment, Mum. And it is handy. And cost-effective. I am a freelance writer, Mum, not a doctor or a lawyer like the Maybury girls. A small place near work is all I need.'

'If you are worried about that Grace girl, I'm sure she can find a new flatmate.'

'I'm not worried about *Gracie*, Mum. I like where I live. That's all.' If her mother had known about some of the shockers she had lived with when she had first moved out...

'Just promise me you will have a look with your father when we get back this weekend.'

'Fine. I will have a look.' She had learned it was no use fighting. Better to agree to think about it and then do things your own way. 'I'm at my tram stop, Mum, I'll have to go.'

'Are you still catching that horrid contraption? Why don't you let us get you a car? I'm sure your father could find you a lovely little runabout.'

'Mother! I will talk to you later.'

'Of course, darling. Goodbye.'

Kelly hopped off the tram and walked along the foot-path to her apartment. The sea air was invigorating. It always gave her a little spring in her step. But the spring recoiled once she saw Simon sitting on the front steps leading up to her apartment block.

He looked up at the sound of her approaching steps. He stood, burying his hands in his jeans pockets. In the warm afternoon light his skin glowed. He watched her as she closed in on his position and as she approached he licked his dry lips. It was the slightest of movements, if she had blinked she would have missed it, but unfortunately her foolish eyes had been trained on his smiling mouth for several steps already.

The memory of their kiss slammed into her mind and her lips tingled tenderly in response. She had to bite down on them to negate her wanton response. She had known from his parting glance that she had not seen the last of him. Yet. But a twenty-four-hour break would have done wonders for her equilibrium.

'How on earth did you find out where I lived?'

'How did you find out where *I* lived?' he asked.

'You left enough hints, Simon. All I had to do was look you up. But *I'm* not in the phone book.'

'I see. Then would you believe I let providence guide me here?'

The bland look she shot him showed him exactly what she believed.

'Your mobile phone bill was on your desk at work,' he finally admitted. 'It's overdue, you know.'

She decided it best to ignore his comment, just as she had ignored the mobile phone bill.

'Don't you have anywhere better to be?' she asked with forced cool as she swept past him and up to her front door.

He shrugged, the movement so natural and so sexy and she had the feeling her equilibrium was not high on his list of priorities. 'You said to do whatever I pleased.'

'Ha! Like you've ever done what I asked you to do. Besides I *also* asked you to leave me alone.'

And then he grinned and her legs all but dissolved from beneath her. She kept a tight hold of the doorknob for support.

'I chose to listen to one and ignore the other. Forgive me.'

Her gaze flicked to collide full on with his.

Forgive him?

He watched her, his hands buried deep in his jeans pockets, and his chest not stirring. She could have sworn he was holding his breath. And she knew that those words were not as flippant as they had seemed.

Could she forgive him? Just like that? After five years with not a word? His very presence dredged up the utter agony that had preceded all of the wonderful changes in her life, for that she would *never* forgive him.

She left the door open, not exactly inviting him in but the last thing she wanted was a struggle on the doorstep.

She walked up the stairs; there was no lift as the building was too old. Simon walked behind her. She was very aware of how tight her skirt was and tried her best to keep her hips from swinging too much, which was hard considering the height of her heels.

She reached the third floor and sneaked a peek over her shoulder to find him still behind her. 'I have been told I have to invite you to a wedding.'

He blinked slowly, his gaze lifting from watching exactly that part of her anatomy she had been so hoping he'd ignore.

She glared back, her mind whirling with the memory of their kitchenette clinch. The recollection of his hand sliding down to her posterior and using that very leverage to show her exactly the reaction he'd had to her. She shook the thought from her treacherous mind and kept chattering.

'My next column focusses on a serial wedding crasher and you and I are going to crash with her.'

'Are we, now?'

'It's the least you can do. Maya wants the dirt on you and there is no way I am going to give it to her. So come with me, get Maya off my back, and once my next article is done she will have moved on to other things. As, I am certain, will you.'

'Sure. When is it?'

Sure? Of course he would say sure. Why couldn't he have an appointment he had to keep? Why couldn't he be as unreliable as he had been when she really had wanted him to be with her?

Kelly dug through her handbag for her keys. Simon took them from her fumbling hands and opened the door for her, standing back to wave her through with a polite hand.

Minky bounded down the short hallway from the lounge, wagging her whole body in glee. Kelly bent so Minky could leap the short distance into her arms.

'*She* hasn't changed a bit,' Simon said.

Minky stopped wiggling, her gaze shooting to the low voice. She looked at Simon for a couple of seconds, her little button nose sniffing the air, and then began to wiggle in earnest, squeaking and yapping and desperately trying to leap from Kelly's arms and into Simon's. Kelly had to let her go rather than drop her and watched in remorse as she gave Simon the type of welcome that had long since been reserved for her.

Simon moved through Kelly's apartment with Minky wiggling in his arms, and she saw it through his eyes. Mismatched furniture, faded curtains, a prehistoric television, pages of handwritten notes for her next *Single and Loving It!* column scattered across the coffee table.

It sure wasn't glamorous but it was warm and cosy and it was the first place she had ever lived in that really felt like it was her home.

He stopped walking and she almost banged into the back of him.

'I like your place,' he said. 'It has personality.'

He was looking into her eyes and it was all Kelly could do not to drown. She grabbed Minky from his arms and used her as a living shield. 'More so than your place, in any case. What's with the designer minimalism?'

Simon laughed, the sound rippling across the room in such mesmerising waves Kelly had to force herself not to duck out of the way of their charming effect.

'It's somewhere to lay my hat.'

Of course. Why lay down roots if you're not planning to stay?

'Well, it's awful,' she said.

'Fine. I'll move.'

She glared at him, expecting to find his eyes crinkled with humour. But he seemed completely sincere.

'You can knock the place down and build a Starbucks for all I care,' she dared, calling his bluff. 'So what do you want now?'

'I was out for a drive and I ended up here.'

Simon moved into the sitting room and slumped down into Kelly's too-soft couch. Minky leapt to the floor and took up position atop Simon's left foot, looking up at him adoringly.

He glanced at the coffee table and leaned forward to have a closer look. Only then did Kelly fully realise her *Single and Loving It!* notes were on display for all the world to see. Gracie was used to it and even added Gracie-style pearls of wisdom on occasion, but Kelly had no desire for Simon to see one word. She all but leapt over him to gather them up in a scrunched heap.

'You write your stuff by hand?' he asked.

She held her *stuff* close to her chest. 'I do.'

'Wouldn't a computer be easier?'

'Perhaps. But scrap paper and a good pen is more economical.'

She glanced at Simon, who was watching her exhibition with unconcealed interest. His large frame dwarfed the tiny love-seat as he sat there, looking all healthy, and strapping, and gorgeous and making no move to say anything further.

Remembering how that healthy, strapping body had felt slammed against her in the kitchenette at work, Kelly once again felt hot and bothered.

'I'll be back in a sec,' she spluttered as she sped down the hall. She made it to the bathroom in three seconds flat and slammed the door shut behind her. The only door inside the apartment with a lock.

Kelly threw her papers into the dry bath, wrenched the small window open, and drank in great gulps of fresh salty air. Only once she felt less hot and less bothered did she slump on the edge of the old bath and stare at herself in the mirror. Her eyes looked huge. The pupils dark and intense. Her cheeks were flushed and her breathing was ridiculously fast-paced. How could the mere memory of a ten-second kiss bring her to such a state? It had to be the fact the kiss had broken a five-year drought. Nothing more.

Nevertheless, she wished the lock were on the outside and that Gracie would magically appear, lock her in, and hide the key. For a month. A month would be plenty. By then Simon would have to have become bored, or edgy, or have developed itchy feet. Whatever it was that had made him flee five years before would surely strike again. Then and only then would she could come out of the bathroom.

What was he thinking turning up like this? No reason? Just because? Yep. That was so like him. He always did things like that. He was so relaxed, so easygoing, whereas she was always so manic and constantly felt wound up as curly as a corkscrew. Such as on the day he'd proposed.

She remembered the exact words. He'd said, 'I was strolling the boardwalk when I found something I thought you might like.'

She remembered jumping up and down in excitement, expecting a perfect shell he had found on the beach or perhaps a new sculpture he had made from found things at the docks. And when he had pulled out a real live engagement ring, a dolphin wrapped around a tiny diamond, she had almost spontaneously combusted with shock.

Even so many years later, sitting on the edge of the cold old bath, she could *feel* the remnants of that joy. The invigorating hit of oxygen as she had gasped in surprise. The moment of detachment from the whole experience as she'd felt as though the bottom of her stomach had dropped away. The excited flush that had begun upon her cheeks and travelled her whole length until warm and loose-limbed, with her stomach back to its rightful place, she had flung herself into his protective, welcoming arms.

Back in the present, Kelly remembered she too had something for him. Resolve finally kicking in, she left her sanctuary and headed into her chest of drawers in the hall, the place where old papers went to die. She quickly flicked through years worth of tax details and electricity bills until she found what she was looking for: a faded old manila envelope with Simon's name on it.

It had been years since she had seen it. Even holding it brought back horrid memories. Screaming fights with her parents, weeks with no sleep, there were even a couple of round marks in one corner she knew were dried teardrops.

Well, this was the moment that would make all of that pain mean something. If Simon just signed the papers and left without a backward glance, those gruelling years of rebuilding her life would not be for naught.

She took a deep breath and headed back to the sitting room, holding the old envelope in front of her as though bearing a precious gift. And it was a gift. It was the gift of freedom.

CHAPTER FIVE

KELLYISM:
LOVE MEANS YOU WILL NEVER BE LONELY AGAIN?
SINGLE AND LOVING IT! MEANS YOU WILL NEVER
NEED A GUY TO GET YOU THROUGH THE NIGHT.

KELLY rounded the corner and Simon was gone. She baulked. Where was he? She had only so much courage to draw upon and with every appearance and disappearance he ate away at it bit by painful bit. She tossed the thick envelope on the coffee table and headed for the front window to see if she could see him heading along the street and far away, as she hoped.

'Are you looking for me?'

She spun to face the voice and found Simon in the kitchen. He had started a pot of coffee and had used Gracie's percolator—Kelly had only ever worked out instant coffee—and he was raiding her pantry.

He ducked his head out from behind a cupboard door. 'You don't have a lot for a guy to work with, do you? Time for a grocery shop, I think.'

She shrugged. She had no idea what was in the pantry at any given time. 'It depends what you are looking for. If you are hoping to find the way back to the front door then I can point that out very easily.'

She earned herself a stunning grin. She would have to stop encouraging that if she was to keep her land legs.

'I'm looking for ingredients for dinner, unless you already had something planned?'

'Vegemite on toast,' she said before she could clamp her mouth shut.

'I see. I'm glad to see some things haven't changed. You still are not one for the culinary arts, then?'

Kelly shook her head. 'Though now I'm pretty handy with a tin-opener.'

And she was hit with another blinding smile. *Aargh!*

'Well, it looks as though we'll have to have dinner out.'

'Speak for yourself,' she scoffed, thinking of the distinct lack of dollars in her wallet.

'I thought maybe a celebration dinner was in order,' he said, blithely ignoring her protests. He grabbed her denim jacket and scarf from the rack at the door and hooked her keys onto his little finger.

'I hardly think your return to Melbourne is worth celebrating,' she chided, her arms crossed.

'I meant for your new job. But if you're so caught up on my return, well, then, who am I to argue?'

She raised her eyebrows. But he just started to swing the keys back and forth like a carrot in front of a stubborn mule. 'Come on, Kell. It's my treat. I'll buy you a nice juicy salad. With extra oil-free dressing just the way you like it.'

Her stomach grumbled in anticipation and all of her resolve dissolved. The mere mention of food and she became a total hussy. Besides, salad with extra dressing? Ha! That showed what he knew about her. She hadn't been a vegetarian for years.

Kelly's obstinate nature and gurgling tummy got the better of her and she swept past Simon, grabbing the keys on the way. 'Make it a big, juicy steak, medium-rare, and you've got yourself a deal.'

They walked to Fitzroy Street which was lined with enough restaurants to capture any fancy. The rain of the day before was forgotten and a sweltering heat had taken its place. The only constant thing about Melbourne weather was its inconstancy. With the unnaturally warm weather, Melbournites were taking advantage. It was seven o'clock at night, still light, and the footpath streamed with families on bikes and roller blades, couples strolling the boardwalk hand in hand, and people of all ages heading to the beach in droves.

A holiday atmosphere had pervaded the beachside suburb and Kelly could not help but be caught up in the festivities, no matter how much she desperately wanted to keep her wits.

Simon led her to an outdoor table of a well-known eatery. It was perfect. The rich aroma of a mix of cuisines floated on the night air and a jazz trio played a haunting tune a couple of doors down.

Kelly hoped her shrunken stomach would do the meal justice as she ordered appetisers and dessert as well as the steak as promised.

'So you're really no longer a vegetarian?' Simon asked when the waiter had taken their order.

'I'm really not.'

'And you no longer wear your belly ring?'

Kelly glanced down at her bare navel and gave her shirt-tail a little tug, trying to cover herself as much as possible.

'And I no longer live under my parents' thumbs.' She shot him a look from beneath her lashes, poised for the sarcastic comment that would no doubt provoke. But he simply smiled his enigmatic smile and took a sip of his wine.

And I'm no longer a slave to your good looks and charm, she reminded herself. *So don't expect me to fall into your arms after a nice dinner and a bottle of wine as I once would have. Many more things than you can imagine have changed beyond fixing. And thinking of new...*

'That scar,' Kelly said. She raised a hand to touch his right eyebrow but pulled away at the last second, withdrawing it to the safety of her lap. 'How did you get it?'

'Sailing accident.'

'So you still sail?'

'Constantly. I worked my way up in the Hedges Boat Building Company until I felt I could run the place ten times better than old Mr Hedges. So a couple of years ago I branched out on my own. And now Coleman Shipyards is one of the biggest boat-building companies in Australia.'

She was ready to brand him conceited but then he added a small shrug to finish off the story and she knew he felt a mix of pride and bemusement with his rapid success. She felt the same way about her column. She really enjoyed what she did for a living and felt a little guilty about getting paid to do it. But then she remembered the blood, sweat and tears it had taken to get to that point and the guilt melted away. She wondered what trials Simon had had to endure to become the man he was.

Kelly found it hard to mesh the young man she'd married whose life dream had been to build himself a boat one day with this guy who now hired a team of men to do it for him. But the Simon who sat before her seemed so confident in his own skin. In place of his youthful skittishness was an effortless self-assurance. And in place of the adoration that used to reside in his eyes at all times, there was something infinitely more assertive. Compared to dreamy young Simon, this guy knew himself and it was seriously attractive.

'And this all happened in Fremantle?' she asked, reminding herself why the conclusions she was reaching were irrelevant. He had run out on her and lived far, far away, for such a long time. Without a word. And without a care for her.

He nodded. 'Though I have been looking into starting up a division here in Melbourne. I have been weighing up certain factors and may even decide to base myself here from now on.'

His warm gaze kept steady on hers and she could not have dragged her eyes away if her life had depended on it. And she had the nagging feeling that in no small way it did.

'Any luck on that front?' she asked before taking a much-needed sip of the delicious wine.

'Let's say I'm still in negotiations. But I promise you'll know as soon as I do.'

'No need, I'm sure. It's hardly fodder for my column so you may as well keep it to yourself. And speaking of my column, I have been told to dig for dirt. Maya also wants to know if you're…seeing anyone.'

The corner of Simon's mouth twitched and Kelly had the terrible sense that her question flipped a switch in his mind. If he had been merely attentive before, he was now entirely focussed on her. And when he decided to turn it on she knew she had better be ready for him.

'Maya wants to know, does she?'

'Straight from the horse's mouth,' Kelly promised.

Though despite herself she wanted to know, desperately. 'So, have you been seeing anyone?'

'Not recently, no.'

Not recently? Well, that hardly cleared *anything* up!

'How about you?' he asked.

'You don't get to ask that as you don't have an editor who wants to know.'

'Nevertheless…' he said, his voice deepening, coaxing, irresistible.

She tried to swallow down the awareness that rose inside her.

She racked her brain to remember the name of the last guy she had almost dated, but that had been six months before and had never gone past a very disturbing phone call during which the guy had continuously put her on hold as he'd been insistent there'd been a prowler outside his house. And she could hardly tell Simon she had almost dated someone she remembered only as Mad Max.

So all she said was, 'Not recently, no.'

He nodded and a flicker of hope flared inside her that he was as unsatisfied by that response as she had been. And hope was a dangerous sign. Kelly could have kissed the waiter when he brought out their first course.

Her entrée was delicious, her steak was tender, and the chocolate mousse was heaven. By the end of the meal Kelly was truly glad she had agreed to the dinner. She had not eaten like this in months and she could feel her tummy bulging from beneath her sexy little top. And to top it all off, with the beautiful weather, the lively music, and Simon's surprisingly easy company, it really felt like a celebration meal.

When Simon suggested a walk to settle dinner, Kelly found she was not yet ready for the evening to end.

The sun had finally set but the city was still shrouded in a stifling heat. Under the glow of makeshift floodlights, multi-coloured towels decorated the sand. And in the distance, between the curved beach and the city skyline, a multitude of boats bobbed up and down in their slips, their wet hulls glinting like fairy lights on the moonlit bay.

Kelly and Simon, walking along the footpath, were drawn to the boats, their glittering beauty like a beacon, a reflection of their past together.

A teenager sailed past on roller blades and Kelly had to leap out of the way and all but into Simon's arms so as not to be taken out. He grabbed her, his arms encircling her around the torso. Long after the boy had passed, Simon had still not let go.

Kelly was forced to turn to face him, her lips only inches from his. 'Thanks, Simon. I appreciate the whole…dashing hero performance, but I doubt he's doing a U-turn and heading back this way to finish the job.'

But all he did was smile. And if she hadn't felt warm in his arms already, that smile was enough for her to light up from within.

'So you can let go of me now,' she clarified, her voice suddenly husky.

Simon released her from his strong embrace, and even though the night was humid she felt cold in all the spots where his arms had been. But he did not completely let her go. One arm remained draped around her waist, his fingers tucked beneath her denim jacket and splayed lightly across her hip.

'Just in case he *is* doing a U-turn,' Simon explained, a cheeky grin tugging at the corner of his oh-so-close mouth. 'You remember how these infrequent hot nights can send sane people around the bend. They can make people do the most unusual things that in the light of day would seem preposterous or in the least downright dangerous.'

She decided it best not to respond as she knew exactly what he meant. She had been there herself.

On a night like this she and Simon had absconded with a 'borrowed' boat. They had drifted only a couple of hundred metres out into the bay so as to enjoy the beautiful view of the cityscape. And before Simon had even dropped anchor she had stripped down to her bare skin and leapt into the ocean.

Her skin tingled as she remembered the tantalising sensation of warm water on the surface and the chill water only inches beneath. The fear factor of the pitch-black depths had only added to the exhilaration of the experience. And then Simon's hand had reached down from the side of the boat, drawing her back on board, her body slick with seawater. Simon had drawn her into his young arms and onto the deck where he had laid out a quilt and pillows. And there under the moonlight they had made love for the first time.

Her first time.

It had been magical. It had been so romantic. And less than a month later it had all been over. And in the five years since that perfect moment, she had never been with another man. She had avoided their attentions, their invitations, and their kisses.

And now she was walking along a moonlit path with a man's arm draped protectively, provocatively around her waist. And it was not just any man, it was her only man and, no matter the great gaping gulf of recrimination and mistrust between them, it felt so good. She found herself tumbling back into that constant ache of awareness that had been the mainstay of her youth. And though the danger, and the heartbreak, screamed out to her, Kelly knew she would feel much worse with Simon's arm gone than with it remaining, so she kept her peace.

As one they turned and headed back and not a word passed between them as Kelly soaked in the beauty, the gentle quiet, the romance of the night. She swam in enchanting memories and enjoyed the new ones that second by precious second were overlapping the old.

It was almost eleven o'clock by the time they reached Kelly's apartment block. Dinner had been well and truly walked off, as had a good portion of the carefully constructed animosity Kelly had felt towards Simon. He led her to a row of cars parked on the street and stopped by a gleaming, immaculately restored 1962 EK Holden.

'This is you?' she asked, surprised. She would have expected something new and flash.

'Yep.'

He ran his spare hand over its burgundy bonnet. Under the streetlamps it was all smooth, sturdy curves, elegant leather and wood trim. Old yet new again.

'This is my mate, Harry,' he said. 'I drove him over from Fremantle. Isn't he a beauty?'

'You drove from Fremantle to Melbourne? That must have taken days.' Through miles of isolated, desolate terrain. 'Are you nuts?'

'No. Just determined. With a need for some solid thinking time.'

Kelly glanced at him but he was still watching his car with that untroubled smile on his face. The air felt thick and she knew it was not the humidity. Kelly finally extricated herself from Simon's light grasp.

'Well, thanks for the dinner. It was...kind of you.'

His gaze swept from his car to her face and she sucked in a gasp of air at the blatant desire blazing across his eyes. And she knew that his thoughts had long since been along the same lines as her own.

'Any time,' he said and she knew he meant it.

He leaned in and took Kelly by the arm, drawing her to him as he planted a kiss on her cheek, just above the corner of her mouth. His kiss was warm and soft and not goodbye. It was full of the promise that he was simply marking his place.

He hopped into the car and wound down the window.

'So you'll call me to let me know about the wedding?'

She was stumped. *The wedding? What wedding? Whose wedding?*

'I've never crashed a wedding before so I'm not sure about the protocol.'

Oh, that wedding!

'Sure. I'll have Judy call and give you the details.'

She could see him pause and she knew he was about to suggest she could make that call on her own, but for some reason he thought better of it.

He gave her the barest nod, gunned the engine and drove away. Kelly watched the graceful car until it disappeared around the corner.

Here she was telling the women of Australia to be happy with their own company and she was feeling bereft the minute he was out of her sight. She was such a fake. And she would be discovered. It was only a matter of time.

She jogged up the steps to her apartment, unlocked the door, threw her keys on the hall table and tossed her denim jacket to its post on the coat rack. Her energy all but sapped after such an eventful day, she shuffled into the sitting room with Minky squirming happily in her arms. She slid down into the squishy couch, hoping she would have the drive to drag herself out of it.

All was still in the house, Gracie would not be home for hours. And Kelly took the quiet moment to think over the night. It had been so long since she had had a night like that. The simple pleasures of a nice dinner and easy conversation with a man. She hugged herself to hold in check all of the good feeling she had rushing through her veins.

The clock in the kitchen chimed eleven o'clock and she had a lot she needed to accomplish the next day. As Kelly rose from the chair her knee knocked something from the coffee table to the floor. She bent to pick it up and found in her hands a faded old yellow envelope with Simon's name typewritten across the front.

The divorce papers that she had not remembered once since placing them there all those hours before.

CHAPTER SIX

KELLYISM:
YOU THINK HE KNOWS YOU EVEN BETTER
THAN YOU KNOW YOURSELF?
THINK AGAIN.

THE next day was Thursday, the day *Fresh* hit the stands.

A copy rested on Kelly's desk when she came into the office that morning. She read the magazine front to back, taking care to read *Single and Loving It!* with as objective an eye as she could. To look at it in context and see if maybe it really was the ramblings of an 'unqualified post-feminist hack spreading easy wholesale answers to serious situations' as someone had once suggested.

It was with a genuine sense of relief that she found it to be nothing of the sort. Though it did perhaps have an anti-male slant, it was all true. The women she had highlighted that week had been through some extreme circumstances that spoke to her and she had the instincts to know they would be mirrored in the lives of many of her readers.

Even so, for the rest of the day Kelly was distracted. She usually yearned to sit down and write. Especially since that fateful cocktail night with her friends when she had discovered *Single and Loving It!* living inside her, the words and ideas had flowed from her fingertips as though she'd been born to write them.

But that morning as she stared at the blinking cursor at the top of the fresh white screen her mind was a blank.

Well, it wasn't blank exactly—in fact it was chock-a-block, but with all of the wrong material. Memories, slivers of the heady days of her youth, were rushing into her mind like an intoxicating slideshow. Long, languorous days at the beach, secret thrilling trysts on the way home from school, delicious kisses that lasted for hours.

There was no doubt about it. She was lit up like a hurricane lamp. Though kickboxing and cocktails had done their job keeping her sexual yearnings in check, they weren't enough. They had been a Band-Aid on the problem, a distraction, another avenue for her suppressed energy but not an alternative. There was only so much abstinence a healthy young woman could take and five years without so much as a kiss were obviously Kelly's limit.

She had lain awake into the wee small hours of the morning, her skin tingling with remembrance of Simon's arm about her waist. If she was getting that worked up over a small caress of her hip, she was beyond her limit!

But why Simon? Why did it have to be him? Surely it had to be just rotten timing that Simon had shown up right on time. She was so stirred up that if a pizza delivery guy had rung her doorbell by mistake she would have thrown herself on his mercy, and then spent hours imagining herself in his arms instead! Surely that would have been the case. A man and a free pizza…how could she resist? Then again, what if Simon had shown up at her door decked out as a pizza delivery boy…?

'Good morning, Kelly,' a cheery voice called from the

other side of her cubicle, thankfully snapping Kelly out of the deep well of fantasy she was again sinking into.

'Hey, Lena.'

'How was your night?'

Delicious. Restless. Unhinged.

'Fine, thanks. Which restaurant are you picking apart this week?'

Lena shrugged. 'Not sure yet.'

'Really? I always thought those review spots were paid for by the restaurants themselves.'

Lena shook her head. 'Most magazines run that way, but not *Fresh*. Maya is an original. When she started *Fresh* it was with the promise that she would not stand for fakes and phoneys. Every word written in *Fresh* must have the ring of truth to it or else she simply won't print it.'

Kelly gulped. 'Is that so?'

'Yep. The readers know they can trust *Fresh*. The advertisers know that if Maya lets them into the magazine, the readers will trust them more implicitly than if they are placed in any comparable magazine. Every restaurant I review well will see an immediate upturn in business. So it's win-win. For everyone. We don't have to write to order and the readers love us for it. I thank my lucky stars every day that I have the honour of working here.'

Kelly hoped her face did not show that she felt her life crumbling down around the wheels of her beloved bouncy office chair.

If any of her fans, the ones who had written in to the magazine in such numbers, found out that the poster girl for singlehood was married and had enjoyed dinner at a romantic restaurant and a stroll along the beach with her husband as recently as the night before, she would be lynched!

She'd only had her perfect new job for two days, she had not even collected her first real pay cheque, and already she was on the verge of losing it all.

'Can you suggest anywhere good?' Lena asked and Kelly just stared back. 'A groovy restaurant on which to shine the spotlight for our punters?'

She sure could. Kelly could almost hear the delightful chatter of happy patrons, the wonderful friendly service, and the taste of the divine chocolate mousse of the night before.

But she shook her head and grimaced in mock disappointment. 'Not off the top of my head. Sorry.'

Another lie. She was out of control!

'So how's your next column coming along?' Lena asked, her eyes bright with excitement. She waved the current *Fresh* over the top of the cubicle wall. 'This week's was the best so far. My friends and I don't make plans for the weekend until we have read it, you know. I've already taken up knitting.'

Lena then held up a very uneven-looking stretch of knitted...something. And Kelly had no idea what she was talking about.

'It's my hobby. Remember around a couple of weeks ago you suggested we get ourselves a hobby? Whenever I find myself craving a night at a club, or feel that ridiculous weak urge to phone my ex-boyfriend, I reach into my bag and knit knit knit instead! And it's so therapeutic.'

Kelly tried to smile back but she was flabbergasted. When she had said take up a hobby she had meant something along the lines of her kickboxing, or a master class, or skydiving. Something exhilarating that could take the place of that rush that women thought could only be filled by the attentions of a man.

Had she really been the one to cause such a vibrant young woman to *knit* rather than enjoy a fun night out? A night out where she would probably meet a guy who would make her all the promises in the world to get her alone on the dance floor, then throw her number away at the end of the night?

Of course she had! No matter how easily men could turn a woman's head or make them feel on top of the world, it would all come crashing down in the end. Always. She knew that in the most intimate way and it was her job to tell the world.

Kelly's smile broadened.

'It's gorgeous, Lena. And I hope, whatever it is you are making, it's for you.'

Lena grinned back. She then grabbed the Yellow Pages and flicked to an anonymous page and picked the first restaurant she came upon. 'Let's give somewhere small and unsuspecting a go this week. Don't you just love the fact that we make such a difference in people's lives? And for the better?'

Lena grinned and picked up the phone. By the look on her face you would think she was ringing to tell the people they had won the lotto. Well, maybe in a way they had.

Kelly looked back to her blank page with renewed enthusiasm and the words flowed as they never had before.

By lunchtime Kelly was starving and her neck was aching. She checked her watch and saw she was running late for her appointment with Gillian, the wedding crasher. She ran into the kitchenette, ate a handful of crackers, sat back down, saved her column, and stuffed what she needed into the designer tote bag she had received as a 'welcome to the *Fresh* family' present from all the girls in the office that morning.

'I was worried I'd missed you.'

Kelly spun around at the sound of Simon's voice and almost fell off her chair in surprise. 'What are you doing here?'

'Judy called to tell me we had an appointment with the wedding crasher this afternoon so I thought I may as well take you as meet you there.'

Kelly could have kicked herself if she'd had the dexterity. She had given Simon's details to Judy and asked her to let him know about the wedding they had planned to crash the next night. Obviously their wires had been crossed and she had given Simon details of the preliminary meeting that day as well.

If only Kelly had been on staff longer she would have wrung Judy's neck. But she somehow figured that would not endear her to Maya and she needed to keep herself in the shadows at the moment. At least until the end of the week when her column was done and she could rid Simon from her life once and for all.

'Fine,' she snapped, trying to plaster a smile onto her face as a wide-eyed Lena pretended not to watch the two of them from the other side of the desk. 'That was very kind of you.'

She grabbed the last of her things and all but bolted from the room. She turned at the doorway and saw Simon was still standing by her desk, introducing himself to her chatty co-worker. She cleared her throat to garner his attention and beckoned him furiously. He waved to Lena, who blushed adorably back, and then he came to Kelly at a saunter.

When he reached her she grabbed him by the sleeve and dragged him from the building. 'Don't you ever talk to any of my colleagues, ever again!'

He held up his hands in surrender. 'She spoke first, Kelly. What was I supposed to do, ignore her?'

'Yes!'

Kelly stopped walking when she reached his gleaming car. It was so conspicuous. You could hardly miss it. She looked over her shoulder having a ludicrous but very real panic that somebody, anybody, might recognise it as having been outside her home for several hours the night before and put two and two together.

Simon casually unlocked the passenger door and opened it for her. She leapt in and slammed the heavy door shut before sinking low into the cream leather seats. It seemed an eternity before he slipped into his side of the car and they were on their way.

'What did you say to her?'

'To who?'

'Lena!'

'Oh. She introduced herself, said how much she enjoyed your column and inquired as to how I was involved. So I explained that I was your husband and most likely the inspiration behind the whole thing.'

'You did no such thing!' Kelly cried out, hoping that he was kidding. If he wasn't she would rip the steering wheel from his grip and crash the car on purpose. Taking herself out at the same time as him seemed not such an unreasonable sacrifice. So long as it would mean he could never ruin her life again.

'Of course I did no such thing,' he said, sending her a beguiling sideways look that did little to slow the beat of her racing heart. 'I barely had time to say *nice to meet you* before you did your chimpanzee impression in the doorway.'

Kelly dragged her eyes away from his calm, smiling face and watched the road. They said not another word until Simon pulled up in front of Gillian's home, which turned out to be a quaint little cottage in the leafy suburb of Armadale.

The neat pathway from the front gate was lined with splashes of brightly coloured blossoms and a family of garden gnomes. And in one corner of the garden, beneath the shade of a huge jacaranda tree, lay a delightful pond littered with floating flowers and lily pads and watched over by a fountain of two playful cherubs. Kelly felt the need to muffle her footsteps so as not to disturb the fairies that *had* to live in such fanciful surrounds.

'Keep your mouth shut, OK,' she whispered as they neared the green front door. 'I don't need you spurting off at the mouth and frightening the poor woman. She could very well be…skittish.'

'By skittish, I assume you mean unbalanced. She'd have to be to write in to your column.'

Kelly turned on him with her hands placed firmly on her hips. '*You* wrote in to my column. So what does that say about you?'

He turned to face her front-on with eyes narrowed and smile widening and Kelly suddenly felt like a butterfly futilely flapping at the fringe of a spider's web.

'Oh, I admit that I am suffering greatly from an imbalance, Kell. But I have recently remembered it's an imbalance that can be all too easily kept under control through regular…attention.'

He took a step forward, his hand reaching out to run down the length of her bare arm, which sizzled with the delicate contact. His heated gaze followed his hand's journey until he had a hold of her hand. Kelly watched, mesmerised as he lifted the suddenly lifeless appendage to his lips, imparting a soft, tender kiss upon her upturned palm.

'Hmm. I feel better already.' His eyes then flickered to meet hers. An eyebrow lifted as though he was daring her to…what? Pull away? Tug him to her?

Her whole body burned under his defiant glance. For fear that she was about to eagerly impart some of that Kelly medicine right there on the suburban doorstep, she whipped her hand away, spun to face the door and knocked using the big brass cherub knocker several times.

'There's a well-known cure for that particular sickness, you know. It's called divorce. I promise you only need to take it once and it won't hurt a bit.'

Before Simon could say a thing Gillian opened the door, and, as an extremely attractive, willowy, redhead in her early thirties, she was as distant from Kelly's imaginings as she could be. And she met Kelly with the most radiant smile.

'Good afternoon, Gillian, I'm—'

'You just have to be Kelly Rockford!'

'That I am,' Kelly said, before being enveloped in a tight hug. 'And this is—'

'Simon Coleman, right? Your fabulous Judy called to say you would be joining us. The more the merrier, I say.' Gillian gave Simon the same big hug and Kelly felt an absurd stab of jealousy hit right behind her navel.

Gillian let go of Simon, then looped her arm through Kelly's, drawing her into the home that was as whimsical as the garden promised.

'I just knew you would be gorgeous!' Gillian gushed. 'I mean, in your photo you look lovely, but I just knew

that you were a good person. There is no way I would
have invited you to join me on one of my escapades
otherwise.'

Kelly thought instantly that here was exactly the type
of reader Lena had described. Someone who took every
word in *Fresh* at face value. She looked around the front
room for signs of knitting but mercifully found none.

'Sit, please,' Gillian offered as she led Simon and
Kelly into her sitting room, which was decked out in a
cacophony of floral fabrics, framed pictures and mismatched wallpapers with illuminated lamps on every
spare surface. But somehow it all worked. The room was
at once stunning, original and comfortable.

Simon grabbed one of the heavy gardening books lying in a pile on the rustic coffee table and pulled a set
of sophisticated black reading glasses from his top
pocket and began to flick through the book.

Glasses? Since when had he worn glasses? And since
when had he picked up a book that did not have a sailboat on the front?

'Did you decorate the place yourself?' Simon asked.

Gillian flapped an embarrassed hand over her face. 'I
would hardly say I decorated it. It's just my stuff, that's
all.'

'It's wonderful.'

Kelly glanced at Simon to see if he was being sincere
and she found him wide-eyed as he soaked in all of the
knick-knacks, mobiles and smatterings of old restored
furniture. He was right, for sure, but she would not have
expected him to even notice.

Gillian headed off to the kitchen to grab some coffee,
leaving Kelly and Simon with the canary in the corner
whistling away happily in its antique gilded cage.

'I wouldn't have thought this would be your cup of

tea,' Kelly whispered. 'Remember I have seen your place.' She did not remember even one hint of colour in his austere apartment.

Simon shrugged. 'As I said, it was just a place to lay my hat. For now.'

Simon's *for now* comment tugged at Kelly's insides like a giant fish-hook. Did that mean he would be leaving soon? Heading back to Fremantle once his business was done? He had promised to let her know as soon as he knew his plans, but did that mean she would know sooner rather than later? The thought took root, and like a resilient weed threatened to loom large in her thoughts for the rest of the day.

'What do you think of this place?' he asked. 'Is this the type of place you would like to live in?'

'I'm quite happy where I am.'

'Sure. I mean, if you had the choice. If you had the budget and the opportunity, what would be your dream home?'

She stared blankly at him. What on earth was he talking about?

Truth be told, she knew exactly what her dream home would be. Ever since she was eleven she had dreamed of one day living on a full-scale version of the *Kelly Junior*, the perfect miniature of the most beautiful sailing boat that had caught her attention and changed her life all those years before. But considering she had terrible seasickness and had only managed her couple of sailing trysts with Simon after having clandestine seasickness shots from her doctor, there was no way she would ever really be able to follow through on that particular dream. But there was no way she was about to tell Simon that.

'What's with the twenty questions?'

'Come on, Kell. What would your dream home be

like? Play a little. What could it hurt to indulge me for once?'

She almost laughed out loud. On any number of occasions over the last couple of days, if she had indulged his every request, whether spoken or silently portrayed through his expressive eyes and tantalising kisses, she had a feeling it could have hurt a great deal.

'Why not here?' she said, deciding to let that comment slide by, untouched. 'Three bedrooms, white picket fence, roomy backyard. Add to that the canary and it's just about perfect.'

He looked deep into her eyes and she had to try hard to keep a straight face. 'Really? Not a three-storey mansion in Toorak? Tennis court? Four-car garage? I am talking no expenses spared here.'

She blinked in response. He had just described her family home, which was the last place in the world she would ever want to live. And *her* Simon would have known that.

The man who sat at her side, looking like her Simon, sounding like her Simon, smiling like her Simon, really did not know her at all. And the heart she had spent so many years toughening cracked just a little at the realisation they had grown so far apart that they were practically strangers.

CHAPTER SEVEN

KELLYISM:
REMINISCING IS A NICE WAY OF SAYING
TWO STEPS BACKWARDS.

GILLIAN reappeared with the coffee. 'I have tea, coffee, infusions, milk, cream, white sugar, brown sugar, cubed sugar, sugar-free sweetener. Please help yourselves.'

Kelly waited for Simon to help himself to a black tea before pouring herself a milky coffee with three sugar cubes.

Gillian did not imbibe; she just sat across from them, on the edge of her seat, obviously thrilled at having such company.

'So,' Gillian said, 'how do you two know each other?'

Simon shuffled in his chair and Kelly leapt to explain first.

'Simon also wrote me a letter asking my opinion on some issues and we have decided to write about him in the column as well.'

Gillian clapped her hands in glee. 'That's wonderful. I am so happy you have men reading your column. I think we all have something to learn from it. Don't you think, Simon?'

Kelly could feel him nodding along beside her and she fought the urge to slap a hand over his mouth. It was only the memory of exactly what he had done the last time her palm and his lips had met that stopped her.

80

Her palm tingled in response. She rubbed the spot with vigour. At least that was one itch she could quite easily scratch away.

'I surely do, Gillian,' she heard Simon say. 'Since meeting Kelly I have learnt more about life and love than I could have ever hoped to know.'

Kelly stopped scratching and her left knee began to jiggle.

'Really?' Gillian said. 'Do tell.'

'Oh, no. Please don't,' Kelly all but shouted out. 'I think we should talk about tomorrow night. There is so much I need to prepare.'

'OK,' Gillian said. 'Tomorrow night turn up at the Ivy Hotel, seven o'clock sharp. Kelly, wear your prettiest dress, and Simon, your most elegant suit. Then we play the night by ear. OK? Now back to you.'

'There has to be more to it than that.' Kelly bit her thumbnail. There had to be another way to shift the focus of the conversation to where it was meant to be.

'Don't be embarrassed by our attention,' Gillian insisted. 'You should be used to receiving such glowing compliments on your column by now. Do go ahead, Simon. Life and love, you said. Please tell me what you have learned.'

Kelly focussed every lick of disapproving energy Simon's way but he seemed to be content to ignore her silent protest. She took a big gulp of her coffee, and scorched her tongue on the hot liquid. This day was not going her way.

'Well, Gillian, since *meeting* Kelly I have discovered the pathway to the heart is a battlefield.'

Simon reached out and patted Kelly's knee companionably and it stopped jiggling at once. But then he let it rest there, his little finger slipping just beneath the hem of her skirt. She drew in a sharp breath and had to force herself not to remove it as that would surely only intrigue Gillian the more. So she just smiled and sat very still as though it were the most natural thing in the world for an interviewee to do.

Gillian seemed untroubled. She just nodded sagely and smiled through it all.

'It has to be traversed with much care,' Simon continued, 'and much forethought. There are so many barriers in your way to knowing someone else's heart and you just have to take them down one by one. Even if new barriers spring up in their place, so long as you have your eyes on the goal, and take it one step, one day, one barrier at a time, you can win.'

'Or maybe you should just yell loud and rush the opposition before they even know what has hit them,' Kelly suggested, finding Simon's comments strangely disconcerting.

'I tried that once,' Simon said, his voice suddenly soft. Kelly turned to face him, she could not help herself. And she found him watching her very carefully, his hazel eyes bright yet earnest in the created light.

'And I figured, this time, deliberation may suit me better. The last thing I want is for the opposition to become wary and duck for cover, as then I might never have the chance again.'

Kelly swallowed down the rising lump that had swiftly hindered her breathing.

Was he really saying what she thought he was saying? Was that what he had been doing this whole time? Not just assuaging a little guilt and sampling a little sugar on the side as she had suspected, but actually trying to win her back?

Kelly's eyes opened wide as she realised she had been

staring sappily into his beautiful eyes for several seconds, during which time his little finger had been moving back and forth, ducking below her skirt and out again, softly caressing her bare thigh.

She leapt to her feet and rushed over to the birdcage. She gripped onto the wires and whistled softly; all the while her heart thudded against her chest so hard it almost drowned out the conversation going on behind her back.

'That's a pity, then,' Gillian said, 'because if the woman you have set in your sights reads Kelly's column there is no way you would get past even the first barrier. Her readers would see you coming from a mile offshore. Wouldn't they, Kelly?'

'Mmm,' she managed to say, 'a mile offshore.'

'So is that what you are going to write about?' Gillian asked. 'Are you planning to warn your readers about the likes of Mr Coleman here with his slick clothes and his charming conversation? Because I certainly think that you should, Kelly. I think this one is a real danger.'

When Kelly's eyes managed to swing back into focus she spotted Gillian's wedding albums—plural—on a bookshelf below the canary cage.

'Oh, thank heavens,' she whispered as she yanked them from their nesting place and held onto them like a lifeline.

She swung back to face her companions. 'Gillian, you simply must clue me in on the stories to go along with these pictures. And don't leave any out!'

They spent the next couple of hours poring over the photographs of the various ceremonies Gillian had infiltrated, whilst Gillian regaled them with stories of close calls and near misses. She was a great storyteller and a wonderful subject for a column. And Kelly was relieved to find she had all the background she needed.

In the late afternoon, when Simon dropped Kelly home and shut off the engine, she knew she should leap from the car the moment it stopped. But she couldn't. Not yet.

Even though Gillian's words rang in her ears. Simon was a real danger. A danger, not only to her job and to the new life she had built for herself, but a very real danger to her heart.

Her heart that was already tender and had never really healed since the last time he'd had his way with it. She had to put an end to it. Whether it was all in her mind or not, she had to stop it now.

She was about to tell Simon that dinner was out of the question, now and for ever, when he leaned over and took a hold of her chin, drawing her towards him and placing the softest of kisses upon her open mouth. His lips teased hers, gently pressing and tugging so that such sweet longing burned in her chest. His tongue barely, briefly traced her trembling lower lip before he pulled away.

Kelly slowly opened her eyes and looked at him, flabbergasted, speechless and liquefied from top to toe.

It was no use rationalising. It was no use pretending. Timing had nothing to do with it. A pizza boy, a fireman, any other fantasy guy would not have held a candle to Simon.

Simon was unlike any other man she had ever known. With a look, a smile, without even as much as touching her he could turn her inside out.

It had been that way since the first moment she had laid eyes on him.

She had been eleven, trussed up in a midnight blue

velvet dress, white tights and patent black shoes, and had run away from home. She had talked herself onto a tram to the beach with plans to stow away on a visiting American battleship.

But as she'd walked the shoreline she'd found nobody to help her on her way but a fourteen-year-old boy, alone with the most magnificent toy sailboat, resplendent with a red hull and brilliant white sails. Mesmerised by the beautiful reproduction that would have been as tall as she, she'd skipped down to the boy and boldly asked what he was doing. He'd taken one look at her and, instead of telling her to go to her room, or keep quiet, or laughing at her for her neat and tidy clothes as some of the local kids would, he had smiled.

He'd happily explained the engineering of the craft, the dynamics of balance and propulsion, and he had not talked down to her as everyone else she'd known did. She had understood barely half of what he had said but had been caught up in his enthusiasm and delight all the same.

By the time he'd been ready to let his pride and joy take her maiden voyage he had christened the boat *Kelly Junior*, and Kelly had been smitten. Long into the afternoon she'd sat on the beach, her chin in her palms, sharing Simon's bread rolls, her fight with her mother and plans to relocate to America forgotten as she'd watched Simon work his way up and down the beach, sending his boat out and catching her on the way in. Only once the sun had begun to set below the waves had he had enough.

Without even being asked he'd caught the tram with Kelly all the way to her home and had walked her to the front door. Then, before Kelly had had the chance to even thank him for the lovely day, her mother had slammed the door shut on his face and bundled her inside and up to her lonely bedroom with no dinner. The only thing her mother had said before turning off the light was that she was never to associate with the likes of *that boy* ever again.

If that wasn't an invitation to trouble she did not know what was, and over the next seven years *that boy* had become the most important thing in her life.

That boy had allowed her to be whomever she'd wanted to be, had led her to the heights of desire, and had been so much a part of the woman she had become that when he'd left she had not even known herself.

But now, five years later, she had rebuilt her life. She had made new friends, developed new interests. She was whole again. She was single, and loving it, for goodness sake!

And now *he* was back, contentedly playing with a length of her hair, curling it around a finger and then allowing it to slip away. Over and over again. He seemed as lost in distant thoughts as she had been.

Then his gaze shifted and locked with hers.

'Invite me up, Kell,' Simon said, his deep sexy voice reverberating through her whole body, heating and melting as it went.

It was such a simple request, all she had to do was nod and she could quench the thirst for him that had all but consumed her ever since she had read his name on that blue stationery.

Who was she kidding? She had the chance to finally conquer the distracting desire that had lain dormant, unsatisfied, since the day he had left.

The day he had left and broken her heart.

'No, Simon. I can't.'

'Will your flatmate be home?'

She shook her head, trying to disperse the pervasive longing that his presence inevitably brought about. 'No, she won't.'

His hand moved from the end of her hair to caress her neck, rendering the most delicious shiver of awareness that made her toes curl.

Kelly's melting muscles warred with her anxious mind and the struggle had her ready to burst. Her heart raced, and she felt the same petrified panic that she used to feel as a kid playing tag or hide-and-seek. But the difference was she was not quite sure whether she was supposed to be hiding or seeking.

She had never been good at the hiding part of hide-and-seek. The pressure always became too much and before long she would rush out into the open and beg for someone to tag her just so the horrid waiting would all be over.

But the last thing she wanted to do was allow Simon to put her out of this particular brand of misery.

'No, Gracie won't be home,' she repeated. 'But it has nothing to do with her and everything to do with me. *I* can't.'

'But you can,' he said. 'All you have to say is, ''Come on up.'' It's not such a big deal. It's just three… little… words…'

Three little words? She had tried three little words a number of times with him with only dire consequences. Compared with 'I love you' and 'Leave me alone', 'Come on up' seemed pretty innocuous. But what would happen from there would be anything but innocuous. It would be life-changing. And she had worked hard to get her life into some sort of balance again. If there was going to be any boat-rocking going on it would not be done by her.

Kelly opened the heavy car door, revelling in the rush of autumn air, which was far cooler than the air they had created between them in the car.

'Goodnight, Simon. I'll see you tomorrow night at the Ivy Hotel, and not before.' She shot him a hurried warning look, then leapt from the car, unable to face any more smouldering glances from his beautiful hazel eyes.

Friday morning kickboxing was a farce. Kelly even stopped bouncing on a number of occasions, her body coming to a complete halt as her mind wandered to thoughts other than physical fitness. The kind you could get in a crowded gym class, anyway.

She then spent all of Friday working on her column at *Fresh*, leaping in fright every time anyone said a word to her, or a phone rang, or a chair squeaked. By the time she got home that night, Kelly's nerves were shot and she prayed for a strong heart as she readied herself for the night ahead.

She arrived outside the Ivy Hotel long before seven o'clock. She had been worried Simon might not have listened to her, as usual, and have attempted to pick her up, so she had organised an early cab and settled in the hotel bar for a couple of steadying drinks. Once one of the regulars became a tad too friendly she moved back outside, waiting around the corner in the shadows of the high trellised fence.

She was wearing the 'prettiest dress' she had been able to get her hands on and was waiting for Simon to turn up in a 'most elegant suit' and she could not help but dwell on the fact that she had never seen him dolled up so before. Even on their wedding night he had not even bothered with footwear to complement his wedding outfit of unbuttoned white shirt and cut-off jeans.

But then again her get-up of a backless black, glittery halter dress—borrowed from a kind and willing Gracie—that draped lovingly over her minimal curves and featured a sexy split from ankle to thigh, and with her hair curled and twisted into a loose chignon, was far finer than her own wedding attire of a white bikini, sarong and flower behind her ear.

Would Simon be standoffish, after the way she left things the night before? Would he be more intent, determined to find another way to break down her barriers? Would he even show up?

'Hey,' a familiar, smooth, rich voice washed over her in the patchy darkness. And, no matter how many 'single and loving it' affirmations she had repeated to herself throughout the night, that voice was enough to melt her from the inside out.

CHAPTER EIGHT

KELLYISM:
DRESS-UPS DOES NOT EQUAL GROWN-UPS.
DON'T BE FOOLED, HE HAS A SLINGSHOT IN HIS BACK POCKET!

KELLY turned to face her husband.

Just as she'd feared he looked movie-star gorgeous, and it took her breath away.

Simon's stylish black dinner suit and classic black tie radiated good taste and probably cost more than Kelly made in a month. Against the crisp white of his button-down shirt his face glowed with good health. His eyes shone as though he knew exactly how affected she was and that he enjoyed the fact very much.

He leaned in to place a kiss on her cheek and Kelly leaned in to accept it, catching a waft of expensive aftershave. It was light, barely there and delicious. She allowed herself the infrequent treat of breathing deep of the picture-perfect moment.

When he pulled away it was not to a polite distance. He remained toe to toe with her and she didn't mind in the least. She simply could not bear to be out of his personal space. Perhaps it was the shroud of darkness, the simple silence apart from the soft rustling of the nearby hedges in the warm night breeze, but the moment felt special and as tenuous as fairy dust.

'You look beautiful, Kell,' Simon said, his subdued voice as disarming as his good looks.

Kelly could not and did not want to control the delicious shiver that ran the length of her body at his words. 'So do you.'

A soft smile touched his mouth. He was so beautiful. So elegant. So self-assured.

Who is this man who has landed on my doorstep? Kelly wondered as she tried to relate the sensations she was experiencing with those she'd felt so many years before. And found that she could not. This was different. This was adult. And this was fast spinning out of her control.

So maybe he wasn't the Simon of old, but nevertheless this was a guy who made her head spin and set her senses on high alert. And that was something nobody else had managed to do to such a degree her whole life. Surely that was not something to be disregarded out of hand.

'How long have you been waiting?' he asked, his voice a caress in the dreamy darkness.

For you? For five long, lonely years. Or perhaps even for ever.

'Not long,' she said, her voice barely a whisper. 'Ten...fifteen minutes. And you?'

He paused and for a moment she thought he was about to echo her silent response out loud. She caught her breath and held it.

'About the same as you.'

Her apprehensive breath released in a slow, ragged stream. If their eyes held any longer she was afraid she would have no choice but to jump him in the bushes. It was either that or explode on the spot.

But before she had to make that drastic choice, Gillian bundled up to them looking stunning in a bright orange taffeta gown with a *matching* jade-green shawl.

'Kelly! Simon! Don't you both look just perfect?'

Kelly sprang back putting a good couple of metres in between herself and Simon. Only once she could feel the night breeze cooling her flushed face did it seem far enough.

'This is going to be *too* easy. Anyone walking by would think you were a young couple in love rather than a couple of tricksters about to pull off a great sham!'

Kelly all but coughed on the shock that rose in her throat at Gillian's innocent words. Her gaze slammed back to Simon in warning not to open his mouth and say...what? That she had hit the nail on the head? Not entirely. She was half right. It was true that Kelly needed for them to pull off the greatest sham in her life; whilst the palpable awareness between them escalated by the second, they simply had to pretend there was nothing more between them than columnist and reader.

Simon wasn't grinning at her, taunting her with his power to tumble her house of cards, as she'd expected. But he was watching her very closely. Intimately. Focussed entirely on her eyes, as though trying to read every minute expression that flickered behind them.

'Isn't this exciting?' Gillian said as she skipped from one foot to the other, obviously unaware of the torrent of electricity zapping through the air around her. 'Nothing like the anticipation, is there?'

Even with the distance Kelly had managed to put between them she managed to hear Simon mutter under his breath, 'No truer words were spoken.'

And Kelly knew for sure that alone in the shadows he had been as close to going for broke and damning the consequences as she had. And though she thought it should have comforted her, to not be the only one going silently mad with frustration, it did not. The fact that they were both on the verge of goodness knew what made it all the more difficult to put it to the back of her mind.

'Come on, guys. We have to do it straight away before you lose your nerve.'

Kelly could sense Gillian bustling about them, but she couldn't move. Simon had not broken eye contact and she was stuck. Stuck in a time warp. Whilst at the same time stuck in the beginnings of something completely new.

'Guys? What are you waiting for?'

For the world to stop spinning on its axis so fast so I can get my head around these feelings!

Kelly swallowed hard, her eyes finally pleading with Simon, her only hope, to take the situation in hand, since he had already proven that, unlike her, he had the power of speech.

With a slight nod, which she knew did not lay their awareness to rest, merely putting it on the back-burner, he smiled and took both her and Gillian by the arm.

'Come on, girls. We have a wedding to crash.'

Following Gillian's gregarious lead, they slipped into the stream of couples edging towards the grand ballroom.

In the bright unforgiving lights of the lobby, outnumbered by strangers a hundred to one, Kelly had no choice but to disregard the magic of the darkness just outside and put her game face on.

Gillian made instant friends with the Jorgensens, the elderly couple ahead of them in line. There was plenty to talk about, starting with how beautiful the bride looked, about how hungry they all were, and how they hoped the bar had champagne on tap.

'Making allies,' she explained under her breath as they shuffled closer to the receiving line.

When the Jorgensens asked whether she was a friend of the bride or the groom Kelly held her breath and felt Simon do the same. But Gillian was a pro. She assumed a most wonderful look of surprise as she spotted someone or other further up the line. She yahooed and waved madly for several seconds then turned back to the Jorgensens, who were by that time quite caught up in her little show.

'What about you?' Gillian finally asked with a big flushed grin. 'Bride or groom?' And the couple happily launched into a detailed history of their friendship with the bride's parents.

Kelly and Simon followed in silence, both with obligatory smiles on their faces as they took a short course in wedding crashing.

Simon laid a warm hand in the small of Kelly's back, giving her a little move on as the line progressed. And there his hand remained, the underlying heat burning through the flimsy fabric of her dress. She knew that if his hand moved a couple of inches higher it would be against her naked back. Work-roughened skin on soft. Latent heat on rising heat. And she closed her eyes and willed it to happen.

But after another little shove his hand slipped away, leaving her burning skin to its own devices.

Finally they reached the receiving line, and Gillian excused herself from the attentions of her new best friends to join Kelly and Simon.

'So are you ready to go the next step?'

Kelly felt herself wavering. The heat, the noise, her besieged mind all threatened to overwhelm her. Add to that the fact that Simon stood so close, all Kelly had to do was shift her weight and they would be flush against one another. But then his hand moved to her back, as though he knew she needed support at that moment. And this time it was skin against skin. Kelly began to tremble.

'I would say we're more than ready,' Simon promised, his voice rumbling against her scorching back. 'So let's do this thing.'

The Ivy Hotel grand ballroom was resplendent. A dozen chandeliers shone their golden light upon round tables covered in ivory lace, upon many liveried waiters, and upon a large glossy dance floor.

The wedding party was already a couple of champagne glasses ahead of the rest of the crowd and the bride and groom had eyes for no one but each other so with Gillian's assurance and Simon's charm, they made it through with no questions asked.

Only once dinner was served did they choose a half-full table and park themselves there. Kelly felt a moment of panic when she realised they had selected the kids' table. A mishmash of pre-teen cousins from both sides had been dumped there like so many leftovers and naturally weren't happy about it. So having three actual adults sit with them made their night. And even if their parents did wonder who the adults were at the kiddy table, they were so thrilled to have the kids not running to them complaining every five minutes they were willing to suspend any concerns indefinitely.

'That dinner was superb!' Kelly gushed after swallowing the last of her delectable cheesecake.

'At one hundred and fifty a head it ought to be,' Gillian said from behind her hand.

Kelly dropped her dessert fork to her tellingly empty plate. 'You're kidding, right?' She did not even have that much money in her bank account.

'Don't sweat it, Kelly. Apparently Great Auntie Mabel and her new toy boy pulled out at the last minute so the food would simply have gone to waste. Think of yourself as a rescuer of good food.'

Kelly looked to Simon, who grinned back as he wiped the last of the dessert from his lips with an elegant linen napkin.

'Do the thing again, Simon!' one of the young cousins insisted.

'What thing?' he asked, his eyes aglow with mischief. Then he proceeded to eat his napkin, only Kelly at his side knew for sure that it was disappearing into his concealed palm.

The cousins went wild with laughter, one of them going so far as to sink under the table he was giggling so hard.

Kelly remembered the way Simon used to have her in fits of giggles whenever they were alone together. It had everything to do with that secret smile, that constant twinkle in his eye. He had always been up to something and she had never been able to read what he would come up with next. Whether he'd been planning to tickle her until she cried. Or tell a really bad joke that would have her groaning in reply. Or tug her into his strong arms and kiss her senseless.

But now, rather than being under the table with the kids, she appreciated his sweet humour for what it was.

After the newlyweds danced their wedding dance, a jazz band struck up and the dance floor was open for business.

Gillian sprang to her feet before anyone else. 'I'm going to find myself a groomsman and I am going to dance until my feet hurt!'

And she was off, to hunt for the most obvious quarry

in the room. Kelly watched her thread through the tables, chatting with anyone who glanced her way. So much for keeping a low profile!

'She's pretty amazing, don't you think?' Simon said.

Kelly staunchly scrutinised the retreating taffeta. Gillian was lovely, even in blinding orange. With her irrepressible energy and her feminine auburn curls piled in a magnificent shaggy muddle atop her head, she was charming.

'She's beautiful.'

Kelly waited in agony for him to agree. She felt Simon pause.

'Sure, she's beautiful, but that's not what I meant. She's more than that. She puts herself out there. She says, *Here I am. Take me or leave me.* Because, no matter what anyone else thinks, she's happy.'

And Kelly knew he was right. She was so interesting because she was happy. She was the healthy version of the *Single and Loving It!* girl. A woman who welcomed love and laughter, problems and pain, as no matter what, she was a woman who lived her life on her own terms.

And that was the moment Kelly knew she was the opposite. The unhealthy version of the *Single and Loving It!* girl. A woman who hid behind her own terms. A woman who gave up the love and laughter so as to avoid even the possibility of problems and pain.

'What are you thinking?' Simon asked.

'Are you saying you're not?' she asked, preferring to skip around the edge of her cavernous thoughts.

'Not what?' he asked.

'Happy?'

She turned to him to gauge his response with as much truth as possible. He was wealthy, he was healthy, and he'd had women ogling him all night. He was, quite simply, a man in his prime. How could he not be happy?

'You know what would make me happy?' he said, not answering the question. But the mild enigmatic smile playing at the corner of his mouth was enough to distract Kelly from her thoughts.

'What?' she asked, her voice more than a little breathy.

'Dance with me.'

Kelly shook her head so hard she felt her curls jiggle. 'I don't think it's a good idea.'

'Come on, Kell. We've come this far without being evicted from the joint. We may as well sample every delight available to us.' The smile now showed a hint of pearly whites.

Kelly swallowed hard. There was no avoiding it. If there was any delight she sought to sample that night it was him. Physically he'd always had the advantage of her; her shameless body was instinctively stirred by him. But the effortless charm he had displayed all night had put more than just her body on notice. Her head felt like cotton wool whilst her heart thumped in her chest as though it were eager to escape its confines and reside with him instead.

She remembered the feeling of being clutched in his arms in the kitchenette at work and knew she could not pass up the opportunity to revel in that closeness again. They were amongst a crowd, and a crowd of strangers at that. What harm could there be?

So she nodded. 'Sure. Why not?'

That earned her his trademark knee-melting grin and she was glad she had a moment to collect herself.

He stood. With one arm casually looped behind his back and the other held towards her. He looked like a prince. A giant amongst men. All class and sophistication. Someone who had garnered ravenous looks from all corners of the room. And Kelly felt a small yet dangerous thrill that the only one he had eyes for all night had been her.

She placed her small hand in his large hand and stood. Her knees did their job and kept her upright. She self-consciously smoothed a curl behind her ear with her free hand and Simon's mouth twitched.

Could he tell she was nervous? Who was she kidding? He knew. He knew her every twitch, every smile, every blink. She could only hope that he didn't remember her regular body temperature as it felt at least five degrees above normal at that moment and it would only spell trouble if he understood the truth of it.

He spun her ahead of him before giving her hand a gentle tug and twirling her back into his arms. His free hand wrapped across her back, and his fingers tucked beneath the fabric at the edge of her dress with such ease, as though it were a move they had performed a million times before.

Kelly was so charged that every sensation was magnified tenfold. The shimmering sequins and gleaming glitter mixed with the vivid swathes of colour of the exotic haute couture evening wear on the wedding guests around her were all but blinding. The mellow music began and she could feel the beat of the double bass pulsing through her veins. Her skin tingled, every portion ached bar the spots where Simon's healing arms wrapped about her.

And they began to dance.

They had danced but rarely in their previous life together. Some basic swaying with arms wrapped tight about each other had been the extent of it. It had been more an excuse to be close than the showcase of any real skill. Yet this guy knew how to hold a woman, knew how to lead, and knew how to sweep her off her feet.

In his sure, snug embrace Kelly felt both beautiful and protected. And the last thing she wanted was for her very image of herself to be so absolutely linked to someone else. She needed to bring herself back down to earth before her sense floated away with her fanciful heart.

'Nice suit, by the way,' she said, with a phoney chummy grin.

Simon slowed their pace and pulled her tight to whisper in her ear, 'It's a rental.'

Kelly had to fight not to laugh out loud as it was so obviously anything but! She pulled away to arms' length so as to give him a lingering once-over.

'Big Bob's Rentals on Bridge Road, right?' she asked. 'Unmistakable lines and that hint of a shimmer from the nylon thread is a dead giveaway. And its colour…navy, isn't it?'

He pulled her close again so that every inch of their bodies that could touch did.

'I believe the precise name is "Midnight Blue".'

'Aah.' Kelly nodded against his shoulder as though this made much more sense. Then her nodding ceased in an instant as Simon's hand travelled the edge of her backless dress from her neck to the dip at her lower back.

'I see you yourself are familiar with Big Bob's Rentals.' He fingered the fabric as though testing its quality, but Kelly knew it was little more than an excuse to run a free hand along her naked skin.

'What, this old thing?' Kelly barely managed to eke out. 'Not so flash as Big Bob's. I found it in the back of the closet and just threw it on at the last minute.'

The song finished. Simon stopped swaying and this time he held Kelly at arm's length. Kelly felt her skin warm beneath his skimming gaze as it travelled the length of her borrowed dress, which left little to the imagination as to her vital statistics.

Finally his gaze raked back to hers, the enigmatic smile now gone and in its place a look of unbridled wanton heat.

'Well, lucky for me,' he said, 'you almost missed.'

There they stood. An arm length away. With Simon slowly caressing Kelly's shaking, outstretched palms. The music may well have started up again but Kelly could hear nothing but the pounding of her stirring heart.

'I'm dropping you home tonight, Kelly. And this time nothing is going to stop me from coming inside.'

After about a minute Kelly breathed again. And she nodded. He was dead right. Nothing and *nobody* was going to stop him.

CHAPTER NINE

KELLYISM:
CRAVING A LITTLE COMPANY AS YOU SIT
ALONE ON THE SHELF?
THINK CHOCOLATE CAKE, AND LOTS OF IT!

SIMON drove Kelly home some time after eleven.

She did not have to invite him up. He just followed and she did not stop him. She knew Gracie would not be home and that Simon did not care one way or the other.

Kelly passed the keys to her apartment door to Simon, who was waiting for them, hand outstretched. He unlocked the door, holding it open for her to enter before him.

There was a note on the floor from Cara to say she had taken Minky for a run on the beach and Kelly could pick her up when she got home. Kelly passed the note to Simon as though he lived there. Without demur he read it before placing it on the hall table below the keys.

'You hungry?' Kelly asked from the kitchen. She opened the pantry door to find it as bare as usual.

'Sure. Why not?'

She glanced up to find him leaning against the doorframe. He had discarded his tie and the top button of his shirt was undone. He looked every inch the sort of man any worrying mother would warn their daughter not to let into their apartment. Her mother had sure warned her enough times and for the first time she thought she understood why.

He had been a beautiful boy who had grown into an exquisite-looking man. And she had not been there to witness any of the transformation. No wonder she found herself turning into a stunned mullet every time she looked upon him.

'What have you got to eat?' he asked, a roguish smile drawing her attentions to his lovely mouth.

Kelly slammed the cupboard door shut. 'I'm not hungry anyway.'

He sauntered over her way, slow as he pleased, and Kelly shrank back against the kitchen sink, gripping onto the bench for dear life. The scent of his woodsy aftershave, warmed from a night of wear and dancing, tickled her nose. When level with her, Simon reached over and opened the pantry door. And as soon as he saw it was empty, the roguish look was replaced with a frown.

'What is going on here?'

'I eat out a lot,' Kelly lied.

'I doubt that. What with the way you scoffed down that steak at the restaurant the other night and the hustle with which you ate tonight, I think those were the first real meals you have had in a long time.'

Kelly rolled her eyes and pushed away from the bench. Her hunger, for food and for him, was fast replaced with defensive anger.

'You sound like my mother!'

'Well, then, she's been talking sense.'

Kelly shot Simon a heated glance. The last thing she needed was for *him* to side with *her mother*! That was like the hawk and the bunny rabbit teaming up. Though she no longer knew who would be classed as which.

'Things have been...*tight* for a little while,' she admitted, 'but that's all changed now. *Single and Loving It!* means I will have a regular pay packet and life will become more comfortable from now on.'

There. Maybe he'd now understand how important the column was to her and back off.

'Comfortable?' he asked as one eyebrow rose. 'And you are happy to settle for comfortable?'

Kelly began to pace up and down the tiny kitchen, which meant two steps, and turn, two steps, and turn.

'Believe me, *comfortable* is a huge step forward and I am looking forward to it more than *you* can understand.'

'Try me.' Simon closed the cupboard door and spun to rest his behind on the bench. He crossed his arms and watched her as she measured the room over and over again.

Kelly turned on him, her ire rising as he leaned back in his expensive suit that would never have seen the dark depths of Big Bob's Rentals. 'You really want to know what my life has been like since…in the last five years?'

'I really want to know.'

Well, he asked for it.

'Fine. The week you left I slept on the beach for a full week until it sunk in that you weren't coming back.'

He winced at the ferocity of her admission. *Good.*

'Didn't you get my note?' he asked, his voice unfairly compassionate.

'Of course I did. But *my Simon* would not leave a note saying he was not worthy of me and was leaving for my own good. That was something my parents would say Simon should do.'

He blushed. He actually blushed. And through the haze of remembered anger and disappointment a truth shone through.

'My parents. What did they say to you?'

'It doesn't matter now.'

'Oh, yes, it does,' she insisted. 'Tell me.'

He gave her a measured glance, then spoke. 'They convinced me that you deserved better.' This time his voice was quiet. Level.

'Are you kidding me? I deserved exactly what I chose.'

Simon stood upright, and uncrossed his arms. Kelly stopped pacing and kept a safe distance.

'No, they were right,' he said. 'I took you straight from your parents' house and gave you too much freedom. It was a rush and you had no choice but to fall in love with the existence I offered. But it would have become very stale very soon.'

'So you left.'

'So I left.'

Kelly's laughter sounded bitter even to her ears. 'Well, they sure didn't get what they wanted from that conversation.'

Simon looked up sharply.

'Sure, they got rid of you,' she continued, 'but though they begged me to return home I didn't, not even for one night. I went from dodgy share house to dodgy share house. I enrolled in university, worked nights and weekends in the most grinding run of jobs, until I earned my journalism degree. Then I hotfooted it around the city looking for real work. Bit by bit I sold stories, one at a time. Bit by bit I made new friends. One night I met Gracie and she had me move in here straight away. I have lived here for over a year now and I am settled. I am happy—'

'You went to university?' he cut in, completely ignoring the rest of her tirade.

Kelly would have seethed if it had not been for the look of pure pride on his face. It was enough to even stop her outburst if she only let it. But she didn't. She couldn't. There was no reason for him to feel any sense of propriety over her. No reason bar one and that was entirely too unbearable to even contemplate.

'As I was saying, I am now happy and—'

'And you are writing a column about how men are the scum of the earth. I think there is one issue you have not yet resolved.'

Kelly spun on her heel and took the few short steps into the lounge. She grabbed the incendiary papers from the coffee table where they had lain dormant for the last couple of days and all but threw them in his face.

'Sign these divorce papers and I will consider it resolved.'

He caught the envelope on the fly and tore it to shreds, the old paper ripping easily in his strong hands. 'I won't do that.'

'Why not?' she cried, falling to her knees to catch the pieces fluttering to the ground.

'Because I want you to give me a second chance.'

It was either laugh or cry and Kelly howled with embittered laughter.

'I can't!'

'You can't or you won't?' he asked.

His smooth, warm voice threatened to turn her mind so she kept her eyes shut tight against his pervasive charm.

'Both. Either. Whichever you'll take.'

He crouched down in front of her and took hold of her bare shoulders. Her eyes fluttered back open of their own volition and locked tight with his. Hazel. Hooded. And more determined than she had ever seen them.

'Kelly, tell me this. In the time I have been gone, the other men you have *known*...' He swallowed and the determination faltered. 'Have you ever felt anything even close to what we had?'

She blinked. What men? The non-date with Mad Max, the man with the imaginary stalker? The one date with Big Ben the seven-foot-tall basketball player with the shoe size bigger than his IQ? The several dates with Goody-Two-Shoes Gareth who held open every door but proudly refused to hold her hand until he had at least met her parents.

A decent slice of chocolate cake had given her more to be excited about than their company.

Even the affection she had for her first beau, Sweetheart Simon, was fast paling into insignificance compared with the torrent of heat and emotion and delight and fear she experienced simply being in the vicinity of the man crouched before her now.

And, considering the years it had taken to get over the last guy she'd felt even a fraction as much for, the thought of having this man build her up and dump her was too much to bear thinking about.

Kelly's fight-or-flight instincts kicked so hard she sat bolt upright and drew on every ounce of courage she had.

'You've said it yourself,' she said, her voice thankfully strong, her gaze steady, despite the fact that Simon was caressing her shoulders with such a tender touch. 'We have both changed too much. I am not the free spirit I once was and you are certainly not the laid-back dreamer. Too much has happened in all those years. We are both more practical now and you have to see how impractical this is.'

'But I can offer you so much more now. I can offer

you a beautiful home. I can offer you the lifestyle you were meant to have.'

'I don't want those things, Simon. I never did. All I wanted was you.'

'Well, I am offering you that as well.'

And she knew he was utterly sincere and the temptation to take him up on that offer was almost overwhelming. But how long would she have him this time? And how would she hope to get her life back on track when her parents, or the offer of a bigger, brighter boat to build, or some sort of misguided selflessness made him leave her again?

She shook her head. 'No. I can't and I won't.'

'Then tell me, Kelly. Tell me what you *do* want.'

Kelly thought of her life as it was now. Of her warm bed. Of her kind and constant friends. Of the new job that gave her a sense of self as she had never had before. Of the *comfort* of her life as it had become.

'Now I want for nothing.'

He looked for a brief flash as though she had slapped him, then his expression closed over. He released her shoulders and he stood. He looked so lost, as if he did not know where to put his hands.

'OK, Kelly. I get it. I guess…I'll see you around.'

No, you won't, she thought. *Now off you go, run away, back to the other side of the country. And this time, please, please, please, stay there.*

He looked from her to the door and back again, before leaving without another word.

As the front door clicked shut Kelly remained on her knees, facing the kitchen sink, her hands full of the scraps of old divorce papers, and her heart aching.

After days of trying to convince herself that she no

longer needed him in her life, it seemed she had at last convinced him.

Moments later a knock at the door drew her to her feet so fast she bruised her knees. Kelly ran and whipped open the door not even beginning to admit to herself what she hoped to find on the other side.

'Who on earth was that?' Cara said as she entered, dropping a huffing and puffing Minky to the floor.

Kelly looked over her friend's shoulder and down the stairs but the staircase was empty.

'Come on, Kelly. Spill. Who was the moody-looking hunk in the dishevelled suit?'

Kelly closed the door. She then unconsciously picked up Minky, who was scratching at her shins, then joined Cara in the kitchen where she was filling the dog bowl with water.

'You know the ex I told you about?' Kelly said.

Cara's wide eyes didn't leave Kelly's face as she put the dog bowl on the kitchen floor. '*That* was him? You are one dark horse, Ms Rockford. I thought you would go for the beach-bum type, not the money man wrapped in muscle.'

Kelly shrugged. Cara was right. The old Kelly had fallen for one and the new Kelly was falling for the other. And the fact that both were wrapped up in the same man was daunting, to say the least.

'So if he is an ex, what is he doing hanging around?' Cara finally seemed to notice Kelly's glamorous apparel. 'Did you two go on an actual date? And if so, wow! And if so, how could you let him go so early? And since you did, I think I understand the long face as he left!'

Kelly bit at her inner cheek as she battled with her answer. But she knew this was the end of the line for her. She needed help. And for the first time in five years she asked for it.

'You must promise this conversation does not go any further than here and now.'

'How can I resist? I promise.'

'Simon was, and is still, my husband.'

Cara stared back and Kelly could see the wheels turning in her sharp mind.

'Does anyone at the magazine know?'

Kelly gave her quick-witted friend a wry grin. 'Nobody knows. Only my parents, who were very happy to tell no one as they barely admit it ever happened themselves. We eloped five years ago. Less than a week later he did a runner and I haven't seen him since.'

'And now he's back?'

'And now he's back.'

'Does he want to reconcile?'

'I think so. Maybe. He says he does but I don't think he knows what he is asking for.'

'And what do you want, Kelly?'

What did Kelly want? The new Kelly was single, and loving it. If anybody read her column that was what they would say. The new Kelly wanted independence and a full life without needing a man to fulfil one bit of it.

But the new Kelly was being visited by old Kelly more and more. And old Kelly lived for Simon. Old Kelly would have thrown everything away just to live in his glorious shadow. And how could those two so very different Kellys even hope to negotiate a decision on what they wanted?

She had no choice.

'I want a lawyer. And I do not want to go through my parents for this one. Can you help me?'

Cara finally gave up trying to be an objective listener

and wrapped her arms around Kelly's small shoulders. 'Sure. I know a great girl. Romy Bridgeport. She's discreet and a total darling. She'll make it feel like a day spa rather than a big ordeal. I'll set up an appointment for you.'

Kelly breathed out hard. The load on her shoulders eased as her friend bore some of the burden for her.

'But since I am sure she is not on call this late on a Friday, and since it would be such a waste not taking this dress for a longer spin, how about I treat you to a double chocolate éclair on Acland Street?'

Even with a chock-full cupboard, that was not something Kelly could say no to.

'Only if we promise not to talk about all of my rubbish.'

'Deal. Though tomorrow is Saturday Night Cocktails. And you know there are no secrets on Saturday Night Cocktails. Gracie and I are your very best friends and we are going to look after you. So be ready. You are going to fill Gracie in and we are going to find a way through this for you, OK?'

Kelly raised a smile for the first time since Simon had gone all motherly on her. She had friends. Good friends. Friends who knew her as just Kelly. Not Kelly the daughter of wealthy parents. Or Kelly the dependent, doting girlfriend. Just Kelly.

Just the way she liked it.

CHAPTER TEN

KELLYISM:
GIRLS AND THEIR MOTHERS. WHAT MORE NEED I SAY?

KELLY woke late Saturday morning. She had slept fitfully with a mind full of contradicting thoughts and her tummy filled with the richest chocolate éclair in town.

Her parents, back from their cruise the day before, picked her up just before lunchtime.

'You're looking a little wan, darling,' was the first thing her mother said as Kelly got in the car.

'Thanks, Mum.' Kelly tugged at her pink knit beanie hat, squaring it over her hair, which was still curly from the night before. Knowing her mother would not like it, she hadn't bothered with make-up in some vague sort of protest against apartment-hunting with her parents in the first place.

'Come on, darling. You know it's up to me to tell you these things. Nobody else will.'

'And that suits me fine.'

'You look gorgeous to me, sweetheart,' her father said when he was able to get a word in. 'Fresh as a daisy.'

Kelly stretched out her seat belt so she could lean forward and give him a kiss on the cheek. 'Thanks, Dad.'

Kelly sat back, breathing in the usual new car smell. Her parents had a new car every couple of years. Always

112

the same make, always the same colour, just newer. The ridiculousness of the fact spurred her on.

'Mother, I have some news to tell you.'

'Oh?'

Something about the 'oh' rang alarm bells, but Kelly soldiered on. 'Simon is back in town.'

'Oh, we know *that* dear.'

Kelly blinked. 'And how on earth would you know that?'

'He called on us just this morning.'

'He what?' She could not have hoped to keep the amazement from her voice. He was meant to be long gone. Packed up and shuffled off to whoop-whoop. His apartment so pristine that his cleaning lady probably wouldn't even notice he had gone.

'He sent a note via courier announcing he would call and then right on the dot of ten, as promised, he came to The House for a visit.'

'And?'

'And it was very nice to see him again. He looks in good health, that's for sure. I remembered him as a skinny sort of fellow. And it seems he has done very well for himself.'

Her mother turned in her seat and Kelly could not believe that she had a little excited flush to her cheeks as she spoke. Her mother who *always* went very pale beneath her make-up and whose mouth puckered to non-existence at Simon's very name was acting like a school-girl with a crush. And then she understood.

'He's *the* Coleman of the Coleman Shipyards in Fremantle, you know,' her mother said in an animated whisper. 'He even made the BRW Rich List last year. Fancy that. Our son-in-law on the BRW Rich List.'

Kelly shook her head to clear the cobwebs that were

fast clogging up her brain. 'Mother, stop! Please. I feel as though I have entered a parallel universe here. So slow down and tell me what on earth is going on. Are you drugged? Did you drink something funny in the water on your cruise?'

'What on earth are you talking about, Kelly?'

'This is Simon you are talking about. *That boy* who I was never allowed to see again. *That boy* who was never allowed in *The House*. *That boy* whose name was never to be mentioned under your roof again.' Kelly slapped a hand against the soft beige ceiling of the luxury car.

Her mother fluffed a flippant wave at Kelly. 'That's all in the past, darling. Besides, he is most certainly not the *boy* he once was.'

'We're here,' Kelly's father said.

Kelly had to remind herself where *here* was meant to be. That was right. They were going to Hawthorn. The Maybury girls' apartment building with its private tennis court. 'Oh, fabulous.'

Kelly's mother waited for her father to turn off the engine and open the door for her before she alighted the vehicle.

Kelly hopped out of the car on her own.

'The Maybury girls live here?' Kelly asked in disbelief as she stared up at the familiar swanky third-storey apartment with its white gauzy curtains flapping in the seaside breeze.

'Of course not, dear. But there is no need to see their place now.'

'There isn't?'

Kelly followed her parents to the front door. Her mother walked up to the buzzer and pushed the button as though she was expected. The door buzzed open and in they went, with her father walking behind her, as though he knew if she saw an avenue for escape, she would take it.

The clacking of her mother's high heels reverberated on the floor whilst Kelly's flat canvas shoes added to the percussion sound with a sluggish shuffle. The lift was already open so the three scrambled inside.

Kelly caught sight of her reflection. So different from the first time she had taken a hard look at herself in those same mirrored doors.

This time there was no slinky black dress, no layer of protective make-up, no haughty expression. There was just a bewildered young woman in faded tight jeans, white Melbourne Zoo T-shirt she'd had since she was sixteen, and a charity shop beige denim jacket. With dark, curled, unwashed hair jutting out of the bottom of a frayed beanie.

Her mother was right: her face was pale, the soft areas below her eyes were dark from lack of sleep. And the hint of colour rising on her cheeks as the lift rose higher gave her away as being nervous beyond belief.

Kelly swallowed down her nerves. This was going to be the strangest day of her life. Her parents taking her to Simon's place. It made no sense. It was alternative universe time again.

The lift doors opened and she followed her parents out into the foyer and for a moment she thought they had come out on the wrong floor. In place of a cool barren apartment she had walked into an inviting home.

In place of the personality-free modern furniture, new overstuffed Jacquard couches in an array of mismatched fabrics littered the lounge. A long rustic table with long wooden benches running either side had pride of place in the dining room. Every spare surface displayed bunches of beautiful Australian wildflowers. Thick piled rugs covered the cool wooden floors.

The once-white walls were now a rich mushroom colour peeking in between all sorts of seafaring collectibles: a life ring, a rustic anchor and dozens of blown-up pictures. There were photographs of the most beautiful sleek sailing boats. And photographs of a dozen Australian beaches Simon must have visited over the years.

And photographs of her.

Kelly forgot her parents at the door as she trailed through the apartment, drawn to the differences like a moth to a flame, her hands reaching out to brush over the glass-fronted pictures as though she could soak up the fond memories through her fingertips. The walls read like a journey through her childhood with Simon.

She had burnt every photograph she owned in her infamous cleansing ritual all those years ago, and seeing copies of those same photos made her realise how ridiculous that had been. She should have cherished them, revelled in them and the joy they represented.

'Look at this one,' she heard her mother say behind her. 'This was the day you chopped off all your lovely hair.'

Kelly came back to the present with a thud. Her stomach knotted as she waited for the chastisement her mother could not help but impart.

'I forgot how cute you looked with that pixie haircut. And so young. So very young. Was I ever that young?'

Kelly spun on her heel to find her parents standing, holding hands, leaning towards the lovely shiny photographs, yet looking into each other's eyes.

'Yes, you were,' Kelly's quiet father said. 'Don't forget I knew you when.' And then he kissed her mother on the cheek and Kelly swore she saw a tear in her mother's eye.

If this was not an alternative universe then at the very least Kelly was still dreaming. She pinched herself hard on the arm but, alas, she was still in this strange beautiful apartment with her parents acting as if they actually wanted to be there.

'Hey, guys. I'm glad you could come.'

Kelly spun so fast she almost tripped over herself.

Simon was walking towards her, a soft, uncertain smile on his face. And though his words encompassed her whole family, his eyes were only for her.

Kelly could feel her parents watching the two of them. But still she could not act nonchalant. She was terrified. She managed to muster up a warning glance, hoping to halt him in his tracks, or turn him to stone or something. Anything other than have him continue his march.

But march he did. Undeterred. Towards her. Into her personal space. Until she could pick up the scent of that same woodsy aftershave and freshly shampooed hair, and as he reached for her she could feel the prickle of the sleeve of his chocolate-coloured woollen jumper and he took her by the arm and leaned in to plant a soft, warm kiss on her waiting cheek.

'Good morning, Kell.' He paused and whispered against her ear. 'Sleep well?'

'Beautifully, thank you,' she whispered back. But she lied and by his crooked smile she knew he knew it too. 'And you?'

'Very well.'

'I thought you would be on a plane to Nowheresville on the other side of the world by now.'

He raised an eyebrow.

'Well, that shows how much you know about me,

then, doesn't it?' He leaned back in so that his breath tickled the curls against her neck. 'Besides, I had the most delicious dream of a beautiful brunette in a se-quined black dress. The things this woman and I got up to would melt your socks off. And it was enough to give me reason to think I should stick around.'

Kelly pulled back so as to shoot him the most deadpan face she could muster. '*Only* in your dreams, buddy.'

'Hmm. Pity.'

He left her to go and say hello to her parents and Kelly had to reach out for the wall to keep herself upright.

'Good afternoon, Bettina,' he said, kissing her mother on the cheek as if they were the best of friends.

'Good afternoon, Simon, dear,' Bettina cooed.

'Thanks for coming, Charles,' Simon said, shaking the older man's hand.

'And thank you for inviting us,' Charles returned, all smiles.

Kelly watched in shock. She felt a scream welling inside of her, but knew if she was the one to break up these strange pleasantries it would only make for a ter-rible afternoon. So she swallowed down her scream and decided to wait and see. To bide her time and watch how the day panned out.

Simon had conjured up a magnificent seafood spread. They feasted on lobster, scallops and Moreton Bay bugs as well as lashings of seasonal stone fruit. They ate with their fingers and left a mess of finger bowls and plates full of prawn shells.

And Simon was the centre of the party. He had Charles shaking his head in amazement at the tale of his rise from carpenter to shipyard owner in Fremantle. He had Bettina enthralled with stories of the celebrities who

had commissioned work from him. And he had Kelly
confused as never before.

He had hypnotised her mother. Somehow. And she
knew it couldn't just be his financial success. Her mother
was not that shallow. The fact she'd frowned upon their
friendship from the start had never been just for the fact
that Simon did not come from money. Kelly's mother
had fretted about his family situation. About his absentee
father, about his wayward mother. Her favourite saying
had been 'the apple never falls far from the tree'.

Yet he now had her in the palm of his hand. Despite
the fact he had done exactly as she had always warned
and left Kelly at the harshest moment possible.

'Thanks, Simon,' Bettina said after they had finished
their traditional Australian dessert of pavlova lathered
with fresh fruit and cream. 'That was a wonderful lunch.'

Charles rubbed his stomach. 'I could do with a nap
right about now. So unless you want me curled up on
your couch for the remainder of the afternoon, we should
hit the road.'

Kelly stood and shuffled in behind her parents, feeling, as ever, like the little girl in the patent leather shoes.

'Kelly, you'll stay, won't you?' Simon asked, his eyes
so full of insistent promise Kelly was mortified that her
parents might notice.

'I don't think—'

'Of course, darling,' Bettina interrupted, all but pushing Kelly away. 'You had no other plans. Stay. Chat.
I'm sure you've had enough of us oldies. Simon, you'll
see she gets home?'

'Of course, Bettina.'

Simon kissed Bettina's cheek, shook Charles's hand
and the small party broke up in high spirits.

Kelly waited by the table. Waiting for Simon to turn her way. To offer some explanation.

He turned. And still she waited.

'So,' he said, leaning in the doorway as she now knew he was wont to do. He pushed his jumper sleeves to his elbows, revealing a heavy silver diving watch and strong tanned forearms browned from years of outdoors work. He ran a hand through his dark hair, which was now dry and softly ruffled, then it slid into a pocket of his brown tailored trousers, which draped from perfect hips to crease where he crossed his ankles. He was so casual and cool, he looked as if he were modelling for some designer's catalogue. He was just that gorgeous. Her racing heartbeat suggested he needed no pizza boy or fireman trappings to ring her bells.

'So what?' Kelly said when she finally found her voice. 'So who were those people who left just now?'

Simon smiled. 'That was a pretty nice normal lunch with the in-laws, wasn't it?'

'That was fighting dirty. It was surreal. And I don't buy it for a second. What did you do with my real parents?'

He shrugged. 'Let's just say that we understand each other now.'

'Well, bully for you. You all *understand* each other and I am left in the dark. What is it exactly that you now *understand*?'

'We understand that we are all in fact on the same page.' He watched her for a few silent moments from beneath lowered lashes. 'All any of us want is what is best for you.'

Kelly threw her arms out to the side. 'And I guess I have no say in the matter!'

She began to pace.

'So you created some sort of bizarre intervention here? And now you think I am outnumbered in your plan for us to give it a second go? Well, you are wrong. This has changed nothing. I have spent the last five years making sure that I am the only one to make that decision. I don't need *them* to give me any sort of blessing and I don't need *you* changing or fixing or *decorating* any part of my life. I like it just the way it is!'

'Don't you like what I did with this place?' he asked and she saw the first sign of doubt she had seen all day.

She glanced around the lovely room with its homey feel and nautical theme and could not lie. 'It's wonderful, and you know it,' she said on a sigh. 'I could not have imagined any home more perfect.'

The apartment conveyed a seamless blend of eclectic cheerfulness and warm elegance. It was the *Kelly Junior* without the need for an in-house doctor to administer daily seasickness shots.

His face relaxed. 'I'm glad you like it. I did it for you.'

'I know! And you're crazy!'

'Not crazy, Kelly,' he said, his eyes all but smouldering his intentions. 'Something else entirely.'

Kelly swallowed. Simon edged himself away from the doorframe, his hands slipped from his pockets and swung at his sides, his clenching fingers the only sign of possible apprehension.

His eyes were all for her, their hazel depths flickering with green flames. Her own eyes dropped a fraction of an inch, seeking out the smooth, flat planes of his mouth. His beautiful lips kicked up at the edges in a slow smile. He knew exactly what she was thinking and obviously liked it.

But she did not. 'Simon...'

'Yes, Kell,' his tantalising mouth said in a deep rumble.

'What are you doing?' she asked as he edged closer and closer, slowly eating up the space between them. She should have moved, she should have run, but her feet were bolted to the floor.

'What do you think I am doing?'

She thought he was going to keep walking until he was close enough to feel her ragged breath fanning his face. And he was not going to stop there. She thought he was going to reach up with those warm, sure hands of his, with their work-roughened palms, and he was going to place one each side of her face. And she thought as a continuation of this one fluid movement he was going to bend towards her, and place his beautiful lips on hers and he was going to kiss her.

And that was exactly what he did.

CHAPTER ELEVEN

**KELLYISM:
IF YOU LOVE HIM, SET HIM FREE.
IF HE WON'T GO, PUSH HIM SO HARD
THE DOOR DOESN'T HIT HIS BUTT ON THE WAY OUT.**

THOUGH each movement was expected, even antici-
pated, the kiss was like no other Kelly had ever even
imagined.

Simon's lips touched hers with such delicacy he stole
her breath away. Every time he pulled those bewitching
lips even slightly away from her bewitched ones, a drift
of his own breath swept across her mouth until it felt as
if she were breathing in tendrils of his soul.

His hands resting either side of her face were deliciously warm. His fingers stroked her temples in exquisite circles, slowly dislodging her knit beanie hat, which
fell to the floor behind her with a soft slap. Then, finding
no hindrance, he buried his fingers in her curls and drew
her even closer, with such tenderness it was enough to
melt her heart.

At some stage her hands stole around his neck and,
raised on tiptoes, she arched her body until it was flush
against his, their warmth mixing and amplifying despite
the thick barriers of wool and denim.

In its own perfect time, the kiss deepened, intensified,
but remained so slow and warm Kelly felt drugged by
its aching indulgence.

Simon lifted her off her feet and carried her to the new blue couch. He lay her down with such tenderness she felt as if she were resting on a cloud. Their lips did not part for one moment before his ample length eased on top of her. She accepted him, entwining her legs through his, slowly, slowly, to be as close to him as she could hope to be.

He shifted his weight and she felt the evidence of his growing desire. Somebody groaned. She did not know if it came from her lips or his, but it sure summed up her mounting torment at having so many layers keeping her from where she desired to be: naked skin to naked skin.

She did not even realise that she was crying until the taste of salty tears became one more disorienting sensation of their beautiful coming together.

After seconds, minutes, eons, of the sweet, intoxicating kiss, a sob escaped her lips. It was a sound overflowing with regret, with longing, with fervent acceptance of what this kiss had given her.

And it was enough to break the spell. Simon pulled away. Far enough that his bright eyes could rove over every inch of her face with a fierce hunger, but close enough that she still sensed it was his breath alone that was keeping her alive.

His thumbs brushed down each cheek, wiping away the telltale salty tracks. He leaned in, placing a soft kiss on each eyelid as though that alone would dry her tears. Then he pulled back and looked deep into her eyes. A ragged sigh escaped his lips.

'Every time I see you it shocks me anew how beautiful you have become, Kell.'

Kelly pictured how she must have looked: ravaged,

with red-rimmed eyes and day-old curls. 'But I have hat hair.'

He grinned and ran a palm over her hair, twisting his fingers into a curl and giving it a playful tug. 'Even so.'

As his eyes watched her curl spring back into place his face held such a look of affection. She had never had anybody else look at her in that way. In fact she had never seen anybody else look at anybody else in that way.

And she knew like a flash of perfect white light that was all at once like the most intense pleasure and the most blinding pain that she loved Simon more now than ever.

It was inevitable. It was inescapable. And it frightened her to death.

She had been under her parents' thumbs through her whole childhood. She had lived under Simon's shadow through her adolescence. And only recently had she been able to claim that she was her own person. And that feeling of knowing herself and liking herself was so precious. It gave her strength, it gave her identity, and it paved the way for her bright future. And that was not something she was willing to forgo. For anybody.

'Go home to Fremantle, Simon. Let me go. For good.'

'No.' He did not seem shocked by her request. He merely refused it and kept playing with her curls. 'I'm not going anywhere, Kelly. I have officially relocated. I already have projects underway here. I have redecorated my apartment. This is my new base. I will be living in Melbourne from now on. And this time I'm not going anywhere. So if that is what you are worrying about, stop.'

Kelly shook her head. 'It is,' she admitted. 'But only partially.'

'What else, then? What else do I have to do to prove to you that what we have is worth fighting for?'

'What we *had*,' she qualified, lying through her teeth. 'What we *have* is an understandable curiosity about one another. Nothing more. And what we had has been eaten away by too many years apart.'

Simon's gaze meandered back to lock with hers. She could see in an instant there was a lot more going on behind those gorgeous depths than curiosity, but that was just tough luck.

'I'm not giving up on you, Kelly,' Simon said, his voice so gentle she found her resolve dissolving under its enveloping warmth.

'And neither am I.'

And that was the crux of the matter. She was not going to let herself down by losing herself to him again. Kelly pushed Simon away, taking her time to disentangle her languid limbs from his. She then shuffled along the couch until there was daylight between them.

Simon watched her with a careful expression. Then he stood and left the room.

Kelly shrugged to herself. Was that it? Had he finally given in? Was she meant to leave?

The buzzer at Simon's door rang. Kelly waited a few moments for Simon to return and when he did not she sauntered over and pressed the button.

'Hello?'

'Cab for Coleman,' the dismembered voice came through from three floors below.

'OK,' she said, wondering for a moment why Simon needed a cab. 'Just a minute.'

Then it occurred to her that the cab was for her. The cab for Kelly Coleman. She swallowed hard, remembering the thousands of times she had practised that very signature on her school notebooks but never having much chance to actually use it: it seemed Simon was playing hardball.

He soon returned with a large box wrapped in white paper and silver string.

'I have a present for you,' he said.

At first glance it had all the looks of a wedding present and Kelly's stomach sank. They had barely had time to get used to thinking of themselves as husband and wife, they had never even had enough time together to share gifts after their wedding day. And it was all a little too cosy for comfort.

Kelly held up her hands as a shield. 'Whoa. No, thanks. I can't accept it.'

'You have no choice. It's yours.' He placed the package in her arms. It was big and heavy. And intriguing. 'All I ask is for you to open it when you get home. Then you can give it away. Toss it out the window. Give it a sea burial. Whatever you like. Just as long as you open it first.'

He picked up her fallen beanie hat, placing it atop her package, spun her on the spot and pushed her towards the front door. 'I assume that was the cabbie buzzing.'

'It was,' she said, aching to put the package to her ear and shake it. 'But I didn't bring any money with me.'

'He'll take you home on my account.'

Simon reached past her and opened the door, led her to the lift, which was open and waiting. He gave her a final little shove and spun her to face him.

'Thanks for coming today. This day was more important to me than you can imagine.'

Kelly looked up from her fascinating package. 'Sure.'

Then she realised she was in the lift, readying to leave. She had been alone with him for barely ten minutes. She cocked her head to one side. 'Why did you want me to stay, Simon? Couldn't I have just gone home with my parents?'

Simon leaned into the lift, holding the doors open with his strong arms. His face lit up with a dazzling smile and Kelly wished she hadn't asked.

'I wanted to kiss you from the moment I saw the car pull up outside. No, from even before that. And no matter how much your parents may have warmed towards me I thought kissing you like that in front of them may have stretched the friendship.'

'Oh,' managed to escape her open lips as her mind fuzzed over with memory of their intoxicating kiss.

She was about to ask when she would see him again, then clapped her mouth shut. It felt so natural. She was leaving his side and all she wanted to know was when she would be there again. *Never* was the answer she needed, but, by Simon's indulgent smile and earlier refusal to brook her proposition that he disappear for good, she had a feeling she did not need to set a date. She would see him again and probably sooner than she expected. And despite her protestations that that was exactly what she did not want to happen, the knowledge made her glow from the inside out.

Kelly held tight to her package on the short ride home. She clomped up the stairs to her apartment, selfishly hoping Gracie would be out as she wanted to open her present in secret. Tonight was Cocktails Night and she knew that all would be discussed at length at that time, but for today, for now, she wanted the chance to revel in the idea of her and Simon for a little while. To revel in the memory of the kiss. To revel in opening a gift from the man she so unfortunately adored.

She opened the door to a hyperactive Minky, and a note from an absent Gracie.

Maya had called to ask how the wedding crash had progressed. She had expressed disappointment at not having to bail Kelly out of the police station for trespassing. And she had another great story idea lined up for Kelly's current column. A young woman had called the brand-new *Single and Loving It!* hotline to put herself up as a guinea pig in a little social experiment and she would be turning up on Kelly's doorstep at ten o'clock sharp. And lastly Maya could not wait to hear everything about Simon of St Kilda.

Minky followed Kelly to her small bedroom. Kelly placed the package on the single bed before throwing open the curtains. She craved sunshine. Daylight. She needed the world to feel as lit up as she was. And the world agreed. Pale sunshine spilled onto her quilt cover, which portrayed playing dolphins. It was the quilt cover of her childhood and she had sneaked it from home during one Christmas dinner.

Minky leapt onto the bed and sniffed at the string. Kelly plonked down onto the bed at her side and all but tore the curly string from the box. There was a small baby-blue envelope attached. She half dreaded what it would say. And the other half of her yearned to know.

She opened the envelope with shaking hands to find a sheet of baby-blue paper inside. The same paper on which he had written his 'Dear Kelly' letter.

And once again she recognised his elegant script.

Kelly
Hope this helps.
Simon

'Hope this helps,' she read again. Hmm. Hardly the tear-jerking apology or the heart-wrenching declaration of undying love she had half been expecting, dreading, perhaps even longing for.

'Help what?' she asked Minky, whose tail waggled all the harder at the attention. So, intrigued anew, Kelly opened the box, wondering what Simon thought could possibly *help*.

As the gift was revealed she broke into great guffawing laughs so loud that Minky barked madly and ran around in agitated circles.

The big, beautiful box was filled with every brand of two-minute noodles on the market. It would fill a shelf in her pantry, no worries, and keep her from starvation for a couple of weeks at least.

She pulled out a packet, shaking her head in amusement as she checked on the flavour and then realised how light those packets were. Even a boxful would not weigh enough to have made the box so heavy.

So she dug deep, pulling out packet after packet of noodles until they covered her small bed, and finally she hit something solid. Once it was revealed, she sat back with a gasp.

At the bottom of the box was a beautiful, shiny, new laptop computer.

Kelly slowly pulled it from the depths of the box. She ran a hand over the fine sandpaper feel of the lid before flipping it open. She pressed the on switch and watched, amazed, as it purred its way to life. After a few moments, the large screen flickered and the background picture astounded her afresh.

It was a picture of a much younger her dressed in a white bikini and sarong with a flower behind her ear. Simon stood next to her, barefoot in an unbuttoned white shirt and cut-off jeans. The photo had been taken on a disposable camera by the celebrant on their wedding night. With the dark waters of Port Phillip Bay shimmering in the background and their faces lit, not only by the bright cheap flash, but by genuine excitement and love. And whilst Kelly beamed into the camera, Simon's eyes were all for her.

She had never even seen the picture, thinking the camera had somehow been lost during the night when they'd had thoughts of nothing but each other. But Simon must have kept it. Taken it with him when he'd left. Had it developed and kept it with him all of these years.

Talk about playing hardball.

'Hope this helps,' he had said and had bought her a laptop, of all things.

A laptop on which he knew she would more easily be able to write her column.

The column he so vociferously urged her to stop writing.

But the column that he now knew gave her so much pleasure and therefore was encouraging her to write.

The column that she would no longer be able to write if her editor and readers found out she was actually married and every day falling deeper and deeper in love with her husband once more.

It helped all right. It helped Kelly realise that he was not mucking around. He wanted her to be happy and he wanted that to mean being happy with him at her side.

As Kelly sat there, her hand toying with her trembling lips, she burst into tears.

After five years the dam had finally burst. The first cracks had shown during her heartbreaking kiss that afternoon and now she was undone.

Kelly fell sideways onto the bed, half of the slippery

noodles packets sliding out from under her and onto the floor. And she sobbed. Loud, hard, racking sobs. The tears flowed so hard and fast she could not hope to see through them so just closed her eyes shut tight and rode the wave of sorrow. She cried until she could cry no more.

It was a turning point. Make or break time. And it was all up to her. She had some decisions to make and fast.

Continue pretending to her devoted readers or tell the whole truth?

Send Simon on his merry way once and for all or give him a second chance?

Keep her precious status quo or risk it all?

And she wondered how on earth she could even hope to make those sorts of decisions whilst her head was in such a spin.

'Kell-Belle? Are you home?'

It was Gracie. Kelly had not even heard the door open. She sat up, wiping away the bulk of her tears, and looked about for Minky who would usually have alerted her to company, but she was long gone.

'In here,' Kelly called out, her voice thick from crying.

Gracie threw her jacket and bag onto her own bed from the doorway across the hall, then came into Kelly's room. She stopped short when she saw the bed covered in packets of noodles, the laptop with its huge picture of Kelly wrapped in a strange man's arms, and Kelly red-faced and sniffling. And she grinned.

'My, my. Seems Saturday Night Cocktails have not come at a better time!'

CHAPTER TWELVE

KELLYISM:
HAVE A GIRLS' NIGHT IN TO AVOID
THE BOYS' NIGHT OUT.

IT WAS barely sunset by the time they made it downstairs to Cara's apartment. Kelly had discarded her jeans and beanie, had showered away the knotted curls, had straightened her hair and glammed up on the make-up, going all out to cover up the signs of her jag of tears. And she wore a slinky dress, a Versace rip-off that always made her feel pretty special.

Cara met them at the door looking effortlessly glamorous as always, in a vintage black satin number. With her shaggy chestnut bob she looked like a socialite from the 1920s.

For Saturday Night Cocktails they always dressed up but stayed in. The three girls made their own versions of the classics with a few specialities of their own, which were terrible more often than not. It had been during one of the more seedy Saturday Night Cocktails gettogethers that *Single and Loving It!* had been born.

Cara held a tray full of pina coladas, each with its own little umbrella. Kelly managed to crack a smile.

Gracie grabbed a drink and made a beeline straight for Cara's leather couch. 'Keep 'em coming, Cara! I've been hanging out for these all week.'

Gracie was the real siren of the threesome. She was

like a naughty Snow White. Jet-black hair that curled just so about her shoulders, alabaster skin, and her tight red dress showed off curves that would put Barbie to shame. Working in the high rollers room at the Crown Casino, she had a handful of marriage proposals a week. Add to that her penchant for red lipstick and a vocabulary that would put a docker to shame, and she was first-rate entertainment value.

'So, Kell-Belle,' Gracie said after she had sipped half her huge drink, 'considering, as always, what happens during Saturday Night Cocktails stays in Saturday Night Cocktails, spill the goss. Who's the guy and what the hell did he do to have *you* in tears?'

Kelly sat beside her flatmate and discarded her strappy shoes on the floor, tucking her feet beneath her on the couch.

'Tears?' Cara repeated as she settled on the opposite couch. She looked as if she should be drinking a martini rather than the gaudy drink she was quite happily sipping on. 'Did he seriously have you in tears? I'll get Ms Bridgeport over here right now, Saturday night or no Saturday night, if he did anything to hurt you, Kell.'

'Why would she need Romy?' Gracie asked.   Kelly looked from one friend to the other and saw two women ready to scratch any guy's eyes out if she gave the word and it gave her the strength to tell her tale. She filled Gracie in on the details so that she and Cara were now up to date. Well, almost.

'Now tell her about the noodles and the laptop,' Gracie urged.

So she did, *then* they were all on the same page.

'Wow,' Cara finally said, placing her empty glass on the coffee table.

'That's putting it mildly,' Gracie said, her drink also

long since finished. 'What do you need from us, Kell-Belle? A smear campaign down on the docks? Flaming torches at midnight? Tonight I met a guy who owns a bank—I'm sure he would know how to cancel your man's credit cards.'

Kelly had to laugh. 'Thanks, Gracie, but that's probably a tad extreme. But some advice from a couple of old warhorses such as yourselves would not go astray.'

Cara lifted a well-groomed eyebrow. 'Well, this *old warhorse* is going to need some more vocal lubrication if we are going to get you out of this one. Any requests? Sweet? Bitter? Festive? Elegant?'

'Long Island Iced Tea,' Kelly piped up.

'Phew!' Gracie said with a huge grin. She jumped to her feet and rubbed her hands together with delight. 'Going straight for the hard stuff. No wonder we get along so well.'

Gracie followed Cara into the kitchen in a two-man conga line. And Kelly finished off her sweet drink, feeling some sense of normalcy at last with the familiar sounds of clinking glasses and giggling friends in the next room.

The girls soon returned with a tray full of the long, cool drinks.

Cara spoke first. 'So the facts as we have them are: you are an independent woman, a woman on the rise, a woman who has just found the dream job, a woman without strings, with a fabulous flat and a fabulous flatmate, and a husband waiting in the wings to blow all of that out of the water.'

Kelly nodded. 'That about sums it up. So what do I do?'

'First things first,' Gracie said, 'does he still do it for you?'

'Do what?' Kelly asked, knowing full well what Gracie meant but marking time so that she could swell her rising blush.

'Does he still rock your world?'

'Well, we haven't, you know, done…anything for me to be able to know for sure.'

Kelly thought of their few fleeting kisses and knew that was a lie. She did not have to have made love to him to know that it would be as tempestuous as it had always been.

Gracie seemed confused. 'Why on earth not? That would have been the first thing I would cross off the list. See if the cogs and wheels still fit. You're married so there's no sane reason stopping you. Or has he turned ugly or something?'

'Ooh, no,' Cara piped up, a wicked grin lighting her usually serene face. 'He's gorgeous.'

'Drop dead?'

'And then some.'

'Hmm. So why can't you, you know, get him out of your system and then move on?'

Kelly knew that Gracie's idea had merit. But she knew that would simply not work. She knew from experience that in falling into Simon's arms, she would never want to fall out of them again.

'I don't know that I will ever be able to…get him out of my system.'

Gracie still maintained the same quizzical look. But understanding dawned on Cara's face. Cara moved around to sit beside her friend and wrapped an arm about her shoulders.

'Oh, Kelly. You still love the guy, don't you?'

Kelly nodded and Gracie finally caught up.

'Well, bugger me. One of the original *Single and*

Loving It! girls has been hooked from the get-go and even *we* didn't know it. Well, Cara, I guess it's just you and me, babe.'

Cara's half-hearted smile gave Kelly strength that perhaps she was not so alone in her struggle.

Cara gave her another squeeze before standing up. 'I think this calls for another round, don't you?'

Kelly gave her friend a big smile. 'You took the words right out of my mouth.'

Just after ten o'clock there came a knock at Cara's door. The three girls sat bolt upright, or at least as upright as they could after a dozen or so cocktails.

Gracie giggled. 'You two look like meerkats with inner ear problems.'

There was a second knock.

'You should probably get it, Cara,' Kelly said in a stage whisper. 'This is your apartment.'

Cara wobbled to her feet and walked to the door as elegantly as she could. Kelly thought there was a fifty-fifty chance she would break an ankle in her high heels but she made it just fine.

There was a petrified-looking woman on the other side. 'I'm looking for Kelly Rockford. The note on her door said she would be here.'

'Oh, my God,' Kelly shouted as she vaulted over the back of the chair. 'Sherona, right?'

The woman nodded. She would have been a little younger than Kelly and her friends, probably closer to twenty than not. She was dressed in a cute outfit of white peasant top and trendy hipster jeans. She was blonde, sweet, and wore not a lick of make-up.

'Guys, this lovely young woman is Sherona, a self-confessed *Single and Loving It!* girl who is going to be a focus of my next column. As a social experiment Sherona has agreed to go for a night on the town without make-up.'

'Do tell, Sherona,' Cara begged as she led the nervous girl to the comfort of the couch.

'I work in fashion retail and as such wear full-on make-up every day,' Sherona explained in a soft voice. 'But now I find I can't even go to the supermarket without putting on my face. I think it's become a bit of a crutch, not just for me but for a lot of women. So I thought that by doing this I could really help other women through *Single and Loving It!*'

'Whoa, Mama!' Gracie said. 'You're a braver woman than I.'

Kelly glowered at her friend. 'You are very brave and that's why we appreciate you doing this for us, Sherona.'

Sherona licked her lips and tried for a brave smile but Kelly could see she was on the verge of chickening out. But before she could say a word Gracie and Cara cooed and oohed and aahed, enveloping her in their attentive kindness.

'So, for the first time in a long time Saturday Night Cocktails are going to hit the road?' Gracie asked, eyeing Kelly over the top of Sherona's head.

'Sure. If you guys don't mind.'

Cara shrugged. 'What's the point of rules if we can't break them as often as not?'

'Besides I think that our previous conversation topic is well and truly exhausted, don't you?' Kelly asked, nodding towards the newcomer.

Gracie winked back. 'Well and truly. Cara?'

'Dead and buried. So, come on, girls, let's go show this gorgeous young thing how a pack of old warhorses do it.'

* * *

The night turned out to be an unmitigated disaster.

Almost.

'Men are scum,' Gracie admonished on more than one occasion as adorable young Sherona was all but shunned by the men at the nightclub they had invaded. In her hip clothes and with her long blonde hair she had attracted plenty of attention, then as soon as she'd faced the men head-on the harsh fluorescent lights had made her eyelashes invisible, added a layer of shine to her face, and showcased her smattering of freckles. And one by one the men had backtracked, with the sort of expression that meant the product had not lived up to its advertising.

Sherona was on the verge of tears half the night. They consoled her that they had picked the hip club knowing that it would probably have the harshest audience. And trouper that she was she stuck with it. Reminding herself that it was all for the good of *Single and Loving It!* women everywhere even gave her enough chutzpah to try to make the first move with a couple of guys.

Kelly, Gracie and Cara attracted plenty of attention in their glam clothes, which acted as a balance to the experiment.

And Kelly's polite chatter to the men she spoke to through the night turned into a whole different experiment. The place was full of fine-looking men. Eligible men. Successful men. Men in Kelly's peer group. Men with glittering personalities and bucketloads of charm.

Yet none of them appealed to her the way Simon did. He was that much better-looking. That much more charming. That much more in tune with her. Who was she kidding? If she had to build the perfect guy, inside and out, Simon would be he.

And she wasn't really swearing off men for ever, was

she? That wasn't what *Single and Loving It!* was really about, was it? She damn well hoped not. Because if it was, then she was in for a long, lonely life and she would have nobody to blame but herself.

Sherona had not even managed to get one guy's phone number and by the end of the night the girls all felt pretty downhearted.

'We are hardly the big tough cookies we all pretend we are,' Cara confessed as they all caught the last tram home.

Sherona looked over to Kelly as though she would deny Cara's claim. But she could not.

'Not so much,' Kelly admitted, and liked the feeling. She linked her arm through Sherona's. 'I think those guys had no idea what they were missing out on with you, Sherona. You have a lot of class.'

Sherona beamed.

'So did you girls have a good night out?' the tram driver asked.

The girls all looked to Sherona to see how she would hold up. 'Not too bad,' she said and Kelly could see her gaining strength every second.

'I bet you had guys tripping over themselves to dance with you,' the tram driver said. 'I know I would have.'

They all turned his way as one. He was young, he was pretty darned cute, he was flicking glances in the rear-view mirror, and they could tell he only had eyes for one of them. Sweet Sherona, with her shiny face and invisible eyelashes, blushed prettily under the attention.

'What's your name, handsome?' Gracie asked.

'The name's Matt,' he said, and they could see the blush rise up the back of his neck.

'They are even blushing in unison,' Cara whispered to Kelly.

'Well, Matt,' Gracie said. 'This here is Sherona, and I think you may have just made her night.'

'Well, miss, even the possibility has made mine.'

Kelly pulled the rope for their stop. Sherona had a way to go to the end of the line, so they left her chatting away with the tram driver, who promised to walk her home as her stop was his last of the night.

'Thanks, Sherona,' Kelly called out, 'you were a good sport. Women everywhere will be impressed with what you did here tonight.'

She flicked a glance at Matt, whose eyes were all for Sherona. Yep, women everywhere would be more than impressed.

'I'll make sure she calls one of you as well, just so you know she got home OK. OK?' Matt called out of the door as they waved their raucous goodbyes.

'You do that,' Kelly made her promise.

Sherona nodded, her blush still firmly in place.

The tram trundled away and the three old warhorses stood in the middle of the road watching until it rounded the corner.

'Well, well, well,' Gracie said. 'It seems that despite our concerted efforts to quell the tide, love truly is alive and well out there.'

Love is alive and well out there. Kelly remembered seeing those words written on a sheet of baby-blue paper, not so long before. And she believed that they could very well be right.

After leaving Gracie to watch some late-night television, Kelly retired to her bedroom. She was searching for something from the past and this time she did not have to rack her brains to remember where she kept it. She went to her bureau and opened the thin top drawer to find the small velvet ring case that rested deep within layers of her underwear.

Cradling the small simple box in her palm, she padded to her bed and sat down. She rolled the box around in her hands for a few moments, then took a deep breath and snapped it open.

A golden dolphin was wrapped around a tiny diamond. The gold was so fine and the diamond so small, it looked like the ring of a child. So delicate. So fragile. In the end so symbolic of the relationship it represented.

For the first time in a long time Kelly slipped the ring from its velvet bed. She dropped the case into her lap and held the ring at eye-level, allowing the still-burnished gold to glisten in the lamplight.

They had never gone to the trouble of buying wedding rings. They had planned to one day. In the future. So this token had been the one solid symbol of their commitment to one another. And the only thing she had not been able to destroy or discard during her cleansing ritual.

Kelly stretched out her left hand, holding the ring in her right. After only a moment of hesitation, she slipped the band onto her ring finger.

It no longer quite fitted. It was a little loose. She knew exactly how it felt. Her whole life now felt as if it just did not quite fit.

She loved her friends. Adored her job. Cherished her apartment. Everything was as close to perfect as she could have hoped. But still it hung about her shoulders as if it were built for somebody else.

In the five years it had taken for her to reach this point in her life, she had been given the chance to become a woman on her own. Not shaped by her parents or shaped by her husband. But shaped by her own decisions and circumstances. And for that, not only should she forgive Simon. She should thank him.

And despite her most determined intentions, she knew exactly what she needed to do to make it all fit.

She not only had to live her life on her own terms, she had to allow herself the chance to have love and laughter, even if it meant problems and pain would soon follow. Life was not worth living without taking that chance.

It was time for Kelly to put herself out there, to risk it all, to take the chance that she might lose herself. As only then would she truly know if the new Kelly was worth finding again.

It was time Kelly became a healthy *Single and Loving It!* girl.

CHAPTER THIRTEEN

KELLYISM:
THERE'S ONLY ONE WAY TO KEEP YOUR LAND LEGS—
DON'T TAKE THE SHIP AS IT PASSES IN THE NIGHT.

THE sun shone hot for the last time that autumn. And Kelly found she needed the darkest pair of sunglasses she could get her hands on to make it out of the house.

It was late morning when she finally set out to find the Coleman Shipyards in a tight white button-down shirt, jeans and rented yellow gumboots. She had planned on doing a Sherona and going without make-up, but had conceded to a little concealer under her eyes to disguise the telltale signs of her hangover.

The lone, large, silver-bearded, fish-scented *gentleman* at the entrance to the docks had pointed out that her strappy high heels would either send her 'keel over mast' as soon as she hit the wooden docks or would get caught between the planks and she would have to hope some docker would fish her out. So he had *loaned* her a pair of too-big yellow gumboots for ten bucks.

She had a feeling from the grin on his face that she was the most recent in a long line of suckers.

So, strappy heels dangling in her hand, she followed the docker's instructions and eventually found the massive, freshly painted structure that belonged to Coleman Shipyards. It gleamed white and new with a great red stripe running the whole way around its girth. The company name was written in large letters along its length.

The whole area was deserted. It seemed that on late Sunday mornings most people had better things to do than trudge along an old dock, gathering bits of fish on the soles of their hired gumboots. Kelly did not. This was the place she knew she had to be.

The only sign that anybody was about was an open roller door in the side of a smaller building attached to the close end of the massive structure. Kelly poked her head in. It was a small concrete-floored boatshed housing one half-built undersized boat and miscellaneous equipment. There was only one man inside. It was Simon and he had his back to her.

He wore faded, torn jeans, work boots, and a navy-blue bandanna was wrapped around his head. His shirt lay discarded atop on old stool.

The light from the open waterside doorway spilled across the floor, lighting his naked, bronzed torso, which glistened with sweat as he rubbed a handful of sandpaper along the upturned hull.

The tingle of a wind chime drifted to her on the ocean breeze. It would be one of Simon's. He had made dozens in their youth, from wood, tin, fibreglass, shells, always from found things at the beach and around the shipyards. And as the chime settled she heard a soft, soulful whistle from the man before her. He took the key of the chimes and curved it into some secret song of his own.

Kelly watched, transfixed, as the interplay of muscles stretched and clenched across his broad back. A rivulet of sweat ran in a wavy course down his spine and disappeared beneath his low-slung jeans. Faded and torn they might have been, but they fitted him as though they loved hugging his every delicious curve. And she didn't blame them.

The scene was so reminiscent of the times she would join him down on the beach as he'd worked on one ancient, dilapidated boat or another.

But the brawny man before her was so very different from that lean young boy who had first stolen her heart. Not only did he look different, he acted differently, he thought differently, he felt different in her arms. And yet with all of those changes, she knew that she felt more deeply for him now than she ever had.

She decided to leave. This conversation could wait. Another time. A time when he was more…fully clothed would be a much better idea.

Her heavy rubber shoe scraped along the concrete floor. The whistling stopped, and Simon spun around.

His muscular chest rose and fell as he watched her from behind a pair of heavy-duty sunglasses. He hadn't shaved since the day before and dark, seductive stubble shadowed his cheeks and chin.

He was so damn sexy it made her ache.

He threw the sandpaper onto the pile of sawdust on the floor. His large padded gloves soon followed. He pulled his sunglasses from his face and tucked the arm into the low-slung waistband of his jeans.

Then he sauntered towards her. There was no trace of the knee-melting smile. No trace of the good boy from the day before. There was just him. All heat and all male. And coming her way.

Kelly almost tripped over as she skittered backwards. But Simon reached out in time to catch her and draw her inside.

'So for once she comes looking for me,' he said under

his breath, so quiet Kelly even thought she might have imagined it.

'We have to talk, Simon.'

'OK.'

'Are we…are you alone?'

He laughed softly, his eyes crinkling at the corners. 'I sure am. The guys wouldn't come down here on a Sunday even if I offered triple time. I like it though, it means I can have some me time.'

She tried to twist from his hold as a fleeting avenue for escape opened up before her. 'I'm sorry. This can wait. I can go—'

'Come on, Kell.'

Still with a hold of her hand, Simon led her over to the only place to sit: a pile of old mattresses, sheets and quilts that had long since been used to take up paint splatter. It smelt faintly of acrylic and seawater and it swept her back to another lifetime.

Kelly removed her sunglasses, and tossed them aside with her strappy high heels. She looked up into Simon's eyes, and though she did not think he would have had quite the night she had, he looked a little worse for wear.

'So talk,' he said, leaving the way open for her to set the tone of the conversation.

She looked away, and kept her gaze firmly on her too-large boots. She had to get through this and she knew she wouldn't get far if she was looking into his beautifully crinkling eyes.

'I'm scared, Simon.'

'Of me?'

'Of us.'

She sensed him shake his head. 'The Kelly I knew was scared of nothing. She would take on the world to get what she wanted.'

'The Kelly you knew was eighteen. And she thought she knew it all at eighteen. And now I know how little she knew about how things really work.'

Simon gave a small laugh of understanding. 'Oh, how I know what you mean. And now what do you know, Kell? Five years on, with a lifetime of experience, what have you learned?'

'I have learned that the only thing I *do* know is what it feels like to have your heart broken. And I know I never want to feel that way again. Ever. And I will do whatever it takes to protect myself from that feeling.' She braved a glance his way, as she had to make sure he had the gist of what she was trying to say. 'Whatever it takes.'

'And what if I can promise you will never have to know that feeling again?'

'Then I would call you my fairy godmother!'

Simon took Kelly's hand in his and her pulse leapt into overdrive.

'I'm not your fairy godmother, Kell. I am your husband. And if you accept me back into your life, I do promise your heart will never ache again. I will make it my life's mission to protect that beautiful, trusting, overbrimming heart of yours from all perils.'

He reached out and traced the line of Kelly's top, just above her fast-beating heart. Back and forth his fingers played, from the collar at her neck, to the dip where her top button clung to the buttonhole.

'Such a beautiful heart.'

Kelly raked in a deep stabilising breath. Gracie had asked if he still did it for her. And the answer was yes. Yes. Yes! Still. More now than ever. With a featherlight touch he had her blossoming beneath his warm fingers.

His hand moved around the back of her neck, lifting her heavy curtain of hair and running his fingers along its length as it rippled through them. His hand then moved to play with the fine new hairs at the back of her neck.

Her breath caught in her throat as his fingers then found the thin gold chain that hung hidden around her neck. He played with the clasp, then ran his fingers down its length. Kelly waited, breath held, as his fingers trailed its delicate length. She felt the gold slide against her chest as it rose from beneath her top. Then, with a soft bounce, the charm dangling from the end of the long chain lifted from between her cleavage and landed on the outside of her shirt.

Simon's fingers froze.

Kelly's head began to swim. She needed to take a breath or she would pass out. She slowly inhaled through her nose and the encroaching black mist was held at bay.

She could feel Simon staring her down but she could not bring herself to look at him. So she just waited.

Soon his fingers continued their journey along the length of the chain until they hit the obstacle at the end. The ring. Her simple diamond and dolphin engagement ring.

'Kell?' His voice travelled to her on a questioning note so hesitant her heart clenched. 'I thought you said you had lost it.'

'I lied.'

'So I see.'

He played with the ring, holding it up to the light as she had in her room the night before.

'So why on the chain?'

She could feel half of him was radiant with the

thought that she was wearing his ring, and the other half was frustrated that it was hidden.

'It doesn't fit any more,' she said, her voice escaping on a worn out sigh. 'I thought if I wore it on my finger I would lose it. And I couldn't bear the thought of losing you…it.'

'Oh, Kell.'

Their raging emotions coagulated into one pure, synchronised thought and they reached for each other, their lips meeting and burning into a blinding kiss.

Kelly was on her back before she knew what was happening. Simon fumbled with the buttons on her shirt as Kelly reached for the fastening on his jeans. She pushed him away long enough to pull the shirt from her jeans and whip it over her head. The cool gold of the ring soon warmed against her hot skin and she felt it slip beneath her as she settled back onto the makeshift bed.

Simon held himself above her, the zipper on his jeans undone, revealing his boxer shorts. Kelly all but growled at the tempting sight before her. Wriggling beneath him, her eyes firmly on the prize, she undid her own button-fly jeans with a resounding *snap, snap, snap* then yanked them to her ankles. Where they would go no further.

'What the—?'

She and Simon looked to her feet as one. Her jeans were bunched in a knotted mess above her bright yellow gumboots. Kelly let go and lay back down with a thud, her forearm flinging over her eyes.

'Those bloody gumboots!' she screamed out. 'I knew they would be the death of me.'

'If you like, I can finish the job,' a laughing velvet voice rumbled from above her.

She pulled her hand away to find Simon still positioned above her, the muscles of his arms on full display as he held up his considerable weight. She felt his latent warmth radiating towards her in spellbinding waves.

Slowly she nodded.

'Are you sure?' he asked.

She knew what he meant. It wasn't just about helping her remove her ridiculous boots; that was just the first step in what was about to happen. She knew *exactly* what he meant. He meant hot, mind-numbing sex. A little voice echoed in the back of her mind; she *was* married to the guy so there was no *sane* reason stopping her.

She nodded again.

That was all he needed. Kelly waited for her boots to be removed with one fast yank, and then he could *finish the job* with maximum haste for all she cared. She was more than ready.

But Simon had other ideas.

He moved away from above her to kneel at her feet. One by one he removed the ridiculous boots, edging them away from her feet with slow, hypnotising pulls that tugged her body against the bed. Once they were removed she had her first moment of self-consciousness, lying back in her comfortable hangover underwear of white cotton bra and panties, with her jeans around her ankles. It was hardly the most alluring position, or the sexiest get-up.

The urge to draw up her jeans overcame her and as she was about to shrug up her knees and grab the belt loops Simon's hands got there first. They started just above her knees. Just above. Not as high as she would have liked, but high enough to stop her movements dead.

She closed her eyes and gave into the heavenly sensation of skin on skin as his hands ran down her knees, down her shins, moving to follow the shape of her calves and to her ankles where they gathered her jeans and pulled them away from her body, leaving her in nothing but her underwear.

When his hands had been gone for far too long, Kelly allowed her eyes to flutter open. Simon was standing before her, lit by the sunlight slanting off the water and spilling through the faraway door, his strong arms hanging by his sides, his powerful chest rising and falling in slow deep breaths. God, he was a beautiful man.

His hands slowly moved to his open fly. The black mist descended once more and Kelly was glad she was lying down or she would have passed out that very second. And then she would have missed the sight of him shucking himself out of his jeans and all, with agonising deliberation, until he stood before her in all his glory.

So graceful. So athletic. And if she wanted him, he was all hers.

Their first time together came swimming back to her in a flash and with a wide sultry grin she threw him the same line she had all those years before.

'Come and get it, big boy.'

His grin rivalled hers and without further ado he did as he was told.

Hours later, when Kelly awoke, the room was darker and colder. The sun had shifted in the sky and no longer spilled its warm light into the cavernous room. She stretched her beautifully aching form, a great yawn adding to the glorious sensation.

She remembered where she was and what she had done. A lingering smile would not leave her lips and she still felt the imprint of the lovemaking along her whole body. With a groan she rolled over so that she could share her overwhelming happiness, but soon found that she alone occupied the makeshift bed.

Simon was gone.

CHAPTER FOURTEEN

KELLYISM:
YOU ARE NOT DEFINED BY WHO YOU ARE WITH BUT BY WHO YOU BECOME WHEN THOSE PEOPLE ARE AROUND.

THERE was a moment of sheer panic. Kelly leapt to her feet, bringing the old quilt with her as her frantic gaze swept over every inch of the room.

Simon couldn't be gone. He couldn't have made love to her like that, so gently, so tenderly, so *lovingly*, taking her to heights she had never even imagined, and then leave her again. Could he?

Then she heard the melodious whistle. It was faint but it was there. Dragging the old quilt with her, she followed the sound as though it was a foghorn in a storm.

He was outside, sitting on a small grassy spot between the boathouse and the water, dressed again in his jeans and shirt, his feet bare. He was whistling softly and staring at the small waves that lapped at the rocky supporting wall.

'Hey, there,' Kelly said. Her voice was low and sleepy.

Simon turned. Kelly held her breath as she waited nervously for his reaction.

Then she melted as the smile he gave her was full of the same tenderness his lovemaking had pledged. He patted the grass next to him and she shuffled over, clinging tight to the quilt as she was naked beneath it.

'Give me some of that, it's chilly out here.'

Before she knew it Simon whipped open the quilt.

Her squeal alerted several seagulls, who were given a full-frontal flash before they squawked off into the sunset. Then Simon pulled her to him and they were wrapped beneath it together.

She snuggled up to him, taking advantage of his warmth for as long as she could. 'You're not a bit cold,' she scoffed.

'Not now.'

They watched the rippling water together for several silent moments. The light slap of the golden waves was hypnotic. And Kelly revelled in the heavenly languor of the moment.

'Doesn't this feel like it used to?' Simon asked.

'It does.'

As Simon had said, Kelly *had* always been unafraid. Ready to sit out in the open in nothing but a quilt. Since he had left she had lost that spontaneity. It had taken for her to be wrapped in his protective aura to feel the safety to be that way again. As if nothing else mattered but him.

But unlike the girl of eighteen, she knew that other things did matter.

'I didn't come here today for…that,' she said.

'You could have fooled me. Traipsing in here in your sexy get-up like that.'

'Gumboots are sexy get-up to you?'

'You bet. You women can keep your high heels and expensive perfume. Gumboots smelling of fish guts will turn a working man's head before any of that fancy stuff.'

He gave her a tight squeeze and Kelly blushed to her bare toes. She had fought against the past for so long but inklings of the good bits were finally seeping through. Though she had not forgotten for one moment what it felt like to love and to lose that love, she had forgotten what it felt like to *be* loved. It was beautiful, it was sacred, and it was all too rare.

And it was not something she wanted to forget again.

But she also did not want that to be the only thing in her life to give her satisfaction. And there was the rub. She had no idea whether that sort of balance was in her. She was an all-or-nothing kind of girl and she was scared that it would have to be all her or all Simon and the two could not co-exist.

'So why did you come here today?' Simon asked.

'To explain. To thank you for your lovely gift. And to apologise.'

'To apologise?' Simon spun her in his arms until she was facing him. His surprise was genuine. 'The explanation I can handle. The thanks I really do not need. But any apologising is completely out of line.'

'But I have been so stubborn—'

He stopped her with a fingertip against her open lips.

'Stop,' he said, drawing his finger away and replacing it with a warm, sweet kiss. 'Enough. From both of us, I believe. I messed up big time leaving the way I did—'

'No!'

He kissed her quiet again, this time with more force. When at last he pulled away, his eyes were gleaming with laughter. 'Cut me off again and I'm sure you can imagine what will happen next.'

Kelly flicked a glance across the water at the deceptively tranquil shipyards lining the shore, and at the smattering of boats gently bobbing up and down in the water along the way. Her wayward mouth clamped shut. She knew to take such threats seriously. Though she had taken one small step towards spontaneity, she was not quite ready to deal with the consequences of defying that particular warning.

'As I was saying,' Simon continued, 'I have spent every day of the last five years convincing myself that I did the right thing. That the time apart gave us the chance to grow up. To live separate lives so that later on we would not regret not having known different people and experiences of our own.'

Kelly swallowed hard. He was saying all the right things. He had been the elder, the more mature, the more responsible of the two of them and it had taken a huge amount of strength to do what he'd done. He'd taken the hard path knowing it would be better for them in the long run.

'But though my theories were altruistic, I was wrong,' he continued. 'From the moment I walked into my apartment and you were there, standing before me, flesh and blood, not just a vision from my very dreams, I wanted to turn back the clock so as not to have missed a second of the journey that made you the woman you are today.'

He finished in a rush, and Kelly sensed the break in conversation.

'Can I...can I talk now?'

A smile lit his face. 'Or will I give the seagulls a show to remember? No, you can talk now.'

Kelly had to squash down the thought of giving the seagulls that show. The thought was growing on her, the longer she was wrapped in Simon's arms.

'Whatever the outcome, I know now that your motives all came from the right place. You did the right thing,' she said, her voice low.

'What? I'm sorry, I didn't quite catch that.' Simon

held his hand to his ear as though he were hard of hearing.

Kelly slapped him on the arm. 'You heard me, you big doofus.'

'Fine. I heard you. But you can't blame a man for wanting to hear *those* words, again and again. Especially from a woman whose job it is to tell the world that all men are wrong.'

Her job. The happy bubble of yumminess that Kelly had been living in burst with those two words. She looked up at the sun. It must have been after five and she had a huge night ahead of her.

Simon must have felt her drifting away from him as he took a tight hold of her.

'I have to go away for a few days,' he said.

A cold shiver racked her body. She was not sure if it came from his breath against her ear or from a mortal dread that he might not come back.

'If I had a dollar for every time I heard that one,' she said, trying to keep her voice light.

Simon breathed deeply against her neck. 'I have some loose ends to tie up in Fremantle. Some business stuff. Some personal stuff. Some stuff, basically. I am going tonight.'

Kelly nodded, biting her lip to stop from asking what the personal stuff could be. One of those people he had been convinced he needed to experience? Another woman he had stringing along in case she hadn't worked out? Five years was a long time, and just because she hadn't given into the multitude of seriously lacklustre men who had wandered into her path, did not mean Simon had been so virtuous. He was a man, after all. A gorgeous man. A man in his sexual prime.

'OK. Then I'll see you when I see you,' she said,

trying hard not to keep her hopes up or to sink into the mire of depression that suddenly lapped at her toes at the memory of the last time he'd gone away.

The urge to live and let live and the urge to stay and fight warred within her and she could not think her way out of her uncertainty. Not whilst wrapped in Simon's warm arms anyway.

She tried to stand but was all caught up in the quilt. She twisted and turned and her frustration grew as she could not get herself free. Finally she flung off the constraint and sprinted inside the boathouse wearing nothing but her gold chain with the dainty diamond ring feeling like an anvil about her neck.

She was half dressed by the time Simon caught up to her. He flung the quilt onto the bed as a stark reminder of what they had so recently shared.

'I will be back, Kelly.'

'Sure. Of course you will.' Her voice sounded unnaturally sharp. She dressed even quicker, doing up every second button. She tugged on the gumboots and was glad they were too big as they slipped on quickly.

She stood, ran a hand through her messy hair. 'So, have a good trip.' She held out a hand, as though expecting a handshake from a buddy.

Simon had none of that. He grabbed her by the hand and pulled her into his warm embrace. 'A few days, Kell. That's all. And when I come back I hope more than anything we can take up where we left off today.'

He pulled her closer still, one hand at her lower back and one delved deep in her hair, and he kissed her. Kelly closed her eyes and sank into the kiss, giving back for all she was worth. She gave him every lick of pain, of heartache, of misguided hope, of pleasure that she had in her. In case it was her very last chance.

By the time she pulled away she was exhausted. Worn out. Her tired body raging with desire and fear and everything in between.

'Goodbye, Simon,' she said.

'I'll see you soon,' he insisted.

Kelly grabbed her sunglasses and her high heels, then took off. She ran as fast as she could up the dock and was surprised to find the lone, large, silver-bearded, fish-scented gentleman was still in attendance in his little shack.

Kelly dragged off the gumboots and handed them over and was noticeably flabbergasted when he returned her ten dollars.

'Thanks!'

He shrugged. 'They disappear more often than not, miss.'

Kelly shot one final glance at the Coleman Shipyards building far, far away. 'Tell me about it.'

Kelly caught interconnecting trams to make it home by six o'clock. Gracie was at work, so Kelly took Minky for a walk along The Esplanade. The last of the small white tents of the St Kilda markets were being packed up. The chalk paintings on the footpath that would have been fresh and colourful that morning had been all but walked away on the bottoms of hundreds of tourists' shoes. The only people out walking and cycling were locals.

She was back home by seven. She showered, changed, cooked up one of Simon's packets of two-minute noodles, basically found anything to do but that which she had to do. Her column.

She had a night to write it. The hardest thing she would ever have to write.

It had to incorporate eye-opening Gillian, brave little Sherona, and Simon of St Kilda.

The readers of *Fresh* expected her true opinion. They deserved it. And she had to decide if this time they were going to get it.

But Kelly knew she really had no choice. The choice had been made when she'd first clapped eyes on Simon at the age of eleven.

The last flicker of confusion she'd felt fleeing from Simon's arms drifted away and everything became clear. She had no intention of living and letting live. She was not about to let Simon go a second time. She was going to fight for what she wanted. Risk it all and take the consequences. It seemed the only choice for a grown-up to make.

She had to tell the truth. For the Lenas who took every word at face value. For the Caras who were hesitant about starting up new relationships and should not have to go into them with so many rules about what not to do. For the Gracies who cut themselves off from the chance at love as they clung to the *Kellyisms* like a lifeline.

And for herself.

She loved Simon with all of her heart. And she was not being true to that exquisite rarity by saying otherwise.

Whether he returned for a week. For a month. Or for a lifetime. Simon was her love and she was his. And it was time he and the world knew.

She sat on her bed and opened up her beautiful laptop.

It was just so pretty! So new. So light. So much hers. Oh, well, at least it was worth a penny or two, so when Maya read her column and fired her on Tuesday she could sell it to pay the rent whilst she looked for another job!

She clicked on a new Word file. Titled it. Dated it. Her fingers paused over the keyboard.

Her heart was full to overflowing, but not with hate. Not with bitterness. But with love. A love so strong. A love that had grown into something new and all powerful. A love that pressed her fingertips to the keys to write a column that could change her life for ever.

You know that feeling when you wake up after having been asleep for far too long? That's me today. But it wasn't dreams that gave me this feeling but real live people, living real lives. Amazing people who have taught me a thing or two about where my life has been heading.

So rather than messing about with the fun and fluffy elements of the adventures I have experienced, I am getting straight to the crux, to the nitty-gritty, to the heart of what I have learned.

First came the amazing Gillian. Gillian is a woman full to the brim with joy. She lives every moment as though it is the most important she has ever experienced. She takes people as they come, feeding off their delight and sharing her own amazing light along the way. She faces life head-on and soaks up every last second. That was lesson number one.

Then came Sherona. Sweet, shy Sherona who had the guts to face up to a very real fear. Allowing her true self to show in public. And think about it. Seriously, how often do we really do that? How often do we put aside the mask, the version of ourselves that we want people to see, the one we think they will like best, and really let our own true selves be seen?

I was there to witness an amazing show of strength from this wonderful woman who ventured out into the world as herself, only to have person after person try to knock her down. But by the end of the night she sure showed them! In one of the more moving moments of my life, a truly wonderful man showed real character. He saw Sherona as herself and he accepted her without question. So to Sherona and Matt I say good luck, you sure taught me lesson number two.

Next, and most importantly, via a fan letter came Simon of St Kilda, the man who taught me the power of love.

Yes. That was Love. Not Single and Loving It!. Because guys, the truth is, I am in love. And I have been for some time. In fact, for pretty much my whole life. And not with that new cake shop on Acland Street (even though their éclairs are to die for), or a killer pair of Kate Madden designer shoes. But in love with a man. With a real, live, flesh-and-blood man. And that man is my husband, Simon Coleman.

Simon is back in my life after some time away. I could write a book on the whys and wherefores but let's just agree that he went out for milk and was gone longer than I expected.

When I first started chatting to you guys about being single, and loving it, he was still out for milk, and I guess I had a lot of pent-up rage that I thought I had long since expelled. And now my fear is that I may have led some of you on with my thus tainted opinions, problematic as I now admit they were.

Be resolute, I once stressed. Be fearless. Be heard. That's the ravings of someone clinging to the rules rather than to life, if ever I heard it!

And then came the lessons.

Be resolute?

Lesson one taught me to be willing to change. To give in to someone else, to risk it all, as the rewards can be beyond your dreams.

Be fearless?

Lesson two taught me we all have fears. The trick is knowing what they are as only then can you face them.

Be heard?

Lesson three taught me to listen. To listen to my heart. And my heart told me that it was built to love. And to shout that from the rooftops.

I have woken from a self-induced dream and I am damn happy to be here.

So Simon of St Kilda. Or Simon of Fremantle. Or Simon of beyond the black stump. Wherever you may be. I am yours for ever. Whether we are together or apart, I am with you. And I love you.

And to the rest of you gorgeous souls who have given me so much by allowing me the chance to communicate with you, I am so sorry if I have let you down. But even more than that, I am sorry if anything I may have said may have stopped you from finding love. From taking it by the lapels and promising you will never let it go.

Because love is something special. It doesn't have to be everything as I have recently learned, but it can sure as heck be one massive part of your life! You can still be you whilst having a loving man at your side.

So don't be a Single and Loving It! *girl. Be a girl in love. Or be neither, if that's what you really want. Make up your own mind and you cannot go wrong.*

As someone dear to me once said, 'Love is alive

and well out there.' And I for one am ready to let go of my fears and let it into my life.

How about you?

CHAPTER FIFTEEN

KELLYISM:
CHANGE IS AS GOOD AS A HOLIDAY?
A LAZY DAY LYING ON A NICE WARM BEACH IS EVEN BETTER!

KELLY arrived at the offices of *Fresh* magazine early Monday morning. She had been up and dressed since before the milkmen.

It had been just over twelve hours since she had last seen Simon. He was coming back. He said he was and she hoped more than anything else in the world that it was true. She tried to convince herself that she wasn't jealous or frightened but she really was. If only a tad.

Just as it was in Simon's genes to flee at the first sign of trouble, it was in her genes to think herself in circles until it was all gloom and doom. To whip herself up into a self-righteous frenzy until she blamed everybody but herself. So it was up to her to break the cycle or how could she hope to believe that Simon could do the same?

The truth was she missed him. And the truth helped to ease her nerves. It gave her a kind of calm. A knowledge that she was doing the right thing.

As it was most likely her last day on the job, she had taken extra care with her clothes and make-up.

Her long hair was slicked back into a smooth low ponytail. She had kept her make-up light and elegant, forgoing the usual lashing of mascara for just a hint. She wore a pink pencil skirt, melon-coloured top and cream stilettos. Her ubiquitous denim jacket and pink scarf finished the outfit.

She had dreamed of buying a new jacket with her first pay cheque. Maybe something leather. Now that dream would have to wait. But she didn't mind. Some things were more important than a leather jacket. Not many things, but some.

Judy's desk at Reception was neat, tidy and unmanned. The desks in the editorial cubicles were also lacking in personnel but were not nearly so neat.

Kelly wandered past her desk to find a stack of yellow Post-it notes jammed onto a spike. Most likely fun, fabulous ideas for upcoming columns. She ached to know what they were but also knew she should not tempt herself in that way. It would only give her more to stew on once it was all over and she had nothing better to do than lie in bed all day, moping and eating dry noodles.

So she uploaded her article onto her computer, printed out her column, then slipped it into a manila folder.

Maya's office door was open, so Maya was in. Of course. But Kelly was glad. No matter the temptation, she did not really want to leave the column and run.

She strolled to the door and gave it a light knock.

Maya waved a talon-tipped hand without looking up from her magazine. A rival publication.

'Damn, that's good!' she shouted at the pages in front of her.

'What's good?' Kelly asked as she took a seat.

'The recipe for sticky date pudding.' Maya slammed the magazine shut. 'Would you believe they spent the previous six pages espousing a no-carbs diet?'

'I'd believe it.'

'I don't know how they live with themselves.'

Kelly swallowed and said nothing. She knew. You

could do it, you just had to make sure you didn't think about it too often.

'So,' Maya said, her long skeletal fingers forming a steeple beneath her chin, her eyes narrowing as she zeroed in on Kelly. 'Why is my star columnist here so bright and early?'

Kelly flapped the manila folder at Maya. 'Just handing in my column.'

Maya's thin eyebrows raised a good inch. 'Already? You have until five.'

Kelly shrugged. 'I know. But it's done. It's as good as it will be.' And she needed to get it out of her hands before she changed her mind and wrote something inane about fluorescent lighting in nightclubs and the plausibility of bright orange becoming the new black, with her usual anti-men, anti-dating, anti-love mandate.

Maya took a hold of the folder and laid it on the desk. Kelly panicked for a moment that she would read it there and then and she was ready to turn and run for her life. But Maya was not about to put her through that.

'I'm really looking forward to this one,' Maya said. 'I have a funny feeling it will be your most outrageous yet.'

Kelly almost laughed out loud. 'You can count on it.'

'Hmm.'

Kelly pushed herself slowly from the chair. 'I'll be off, then.'

Maya smiled and nodded.

Kelly took a good look around the office, trying to commit to memory the intoxicating scent of day-old Australian wildflowers and week-old newspapers. It was the stuff of inspiration.

'Thanks for giving me this chance, Maya,' Kelly said. 'It has meant so much to me and I will never forget it.'

Then she left without allaying Maya's puzzled expression.

She met Lena on her way out the front door. She had a big white box in her arms. 'Gift from a happy café,' Lena explained, blushing profusely. 'The Pastry Pantry. You will have to help me eat these or I will soon become the very stereotype of a restaurant critic.'

'Lay it out in the kitchenette,' Kelly advised. 'I bet they'll be gone before the coffee machine finishes percolating.'

Lena's eyes lit up. 'What would I do without you around here? Probably become the very stereotype of a restaurant critic,' she said with a big chubby-cheeked grin.

Kelly knew she would miss Lena. But she also felt a great deal of relief that hopefully her column would make a difference in her life. That maybe she would take the hint and learn to make decisions for herself. Then her heart slumped as she remembered the column would not be printed. Oh, well, maybe she would email it to her. And to Gillian and Sherona. They deserved to know what they meant to her.

And Simon. More than anybody else, she had written the column for him. She only hoped that one day, and sooner rather than later, she would be able to share that with him.

Kelly bought a newspaper on the way home and spent a good half-hour in bed circling job ads before falling asleep in an exhausted lump and sleeping away the rest of the day, dreaming of the moment Simon would return and they could take up where they left off.

Tuesday Kelly pulled a sickie. It would usually be the day when Maya would call each writer in for any last-minute edits before the copy was put to bed that night. But Kelly did not hear a peep from her editor. The deafening silence dried up any last hope that she might be forgiven.

No word from Simon. She missed him more than ever before.

Wednesday Kelly had kickboxing class in the morning and for the first time in a long time the bag didn't represent anything or anybody. The bag was just the bag.

But after three days *sans* Simon, Kelly's body was craving his once more. It was no longer satisfied. It now knew what it had been missing for the last few years and it wanted more! The poor punching bag did not know what hit it as Kelly almost jolted it from its chain.

Exercised to exhaustion, she visited her mother. She had lunch in the Toorak home in which she grew up. She dressed nicely as her mother would have wished and even managed to hold a civilised conversation for most of the afternoon.

'I haven't heard from Simon for a while,' her mother finally said between sips of tea.

Here we go, Kelly thought, battening down the hatches.

'He's in Fremantle,' she explained, 'tying up some loose ends.'

'Oh. And when will he be back?'

Kelly shrugged, feigning a sureness she felt less every day he was gone. 'He didn't say. When he's ready to come back, I suppose.'

'And that's OK by you?'

Kelly looked up at her mother's question. She heard real concern there. But not chastisement, or bitterness, or *I told you so*.

'It has to be,' Kelly said. 'I love him. And I want to be with him. And that means giving him all the space he needs to be who he needs to be.'

Bettina seemed to mull that over for a while, then she nodded. 'That seems sensible.'

'It does?' Kelly blurted.

'It does. And that's all I ever wanted for you, darling. To have all the opportunity in the world to become the woman I knew *you* could be. I wanted you to have the time, the freedom, and the chance to have an extraordinary life. That's all any mother wants.'

Old Kelly would have blazed and spluttered that she sure got what she wanted. But new Kelly took a moment and realised that, though it was the woman before her who had helped to send Simon away in the first place, there was only concern and instinct behind her motives.

'Thanks, Mum. That's a really nice thing to say.'

Bettina patted her daughter's knee and Kelly felt all the acrimony of the past several years wipe away with that one affectionate touch.

'So, now that your love life is sorted out, can we please fix this job of yours? I am for ever having to defend you and your little column down at the club.'

Well, thought Kelly, *one step at a time. One step at a time!*

Then on Thursday *Fresh* hit the shelves and Kelly became a shut-in. She kept the phone off the hook and hid under her quilt all morning.

By midday she was starving hungry but couldn't look at another packet of two-minute noodles. She had eaten enough to last her a lifetime.

And she needed sunlight and fresh air. Stuck at home with nothing but her own thoughts she felt as if she were suffocating. Minky thought it was Christmas, she so rarely left the house during the day. She didn't even try to contain her wriggles as Kelly carried her down the stairs and outside.

They walked The Esplanade, Minky stopping to tell every dog that it was daylight and she was out for a walk and how excited she was.

Kelly stopped outside one of the line of cafés with water bowls to let Minky have a drink and realised she could do with some refreshment herself. She reached into the pocket of her tracksuit top and found ten dollars. The last ten dollars she had on earth. She held it out in front of her, with one eye closed and the other zeroed in on the blue note.

She could go to the casino and bet it all on red, win, go double or nothing, and keep winning a few hundred times until she had thousands with which to pay the rent and bills until she found a new job.

Or she could put it in the bank where it would earn less than a cent interest by the time her rent was due.

Or she could spend it on a seriously heavenly piece of Death by Chocolate Cake in the French patisserie right in front of her. And then she would have exactly enough left over to buy a copy of *Fresh* from the newsagent next door.

Was there really any decision? She bought the cake, she bought the magazine and she took a seat. She fed Minky crumbs from her cake as she watched the eccentric St Kilda crowd go by. Groups of young trendies. Rich elderly couples. Daggy Uni kids.

She imagined sitting there with Simon, knowing he loved to people-watch as much as she did. She pictured them sitting there in the sunshine on a lazy weekend, Minky twisting and turning between the table legs until she had knotted the lead and become stuck. She pictured them holding hands, watching each other more than the people around them, and she knew she had done the right thing. Even the mere thought filled her heart with such joy she could feed off it alone for a good week.

When the cake was all gone, all but licked from the plate, she had wasted time long enough.

She opened the magazine, flicked past the pages of celebrities in glamorous dress, past the note from the editor with a picture of Maya looking dazzling in her usual silver, until she reached the point where *Single and Loving It!* would usually reside.

Heart thumping in her chest, she flicked open the page.

And there *Single and Loving It!* was, in all its glory.

Kelly read it all. Again and again. Not a word was changed, not a single word. Tears of joy and relief and shock streamed down her face.

'Why the tears, sweetheart?'

Kelly looked up. She blinked through her tears. And blinked again.

'Simon?'

'Yeah, it's me.'

'Oh, Simon!'

Kelly flung herself into Simon's arms. She stood up so fast she knocked her chair, which crashed to the ground. She kissed his face, his neck, and his face again. Minky was so caught up in the excitement she yapped her little heart out.

'When did you get back?'

'Just now.' He motioned to the overnight bag in his hand. 'I came straight from the airport. Cara let me into your apartment and we found your note to Gracie saying you would be down here. I kind of figured, knowing you, ''Walking Minky'' would mean eating cake.'

Kelly threw her arms around him again. 'You know me too well.'

'Just well enough, I think.' He pulled back and wiped the streaming tears from her face. 'Are you OK? I mean, you are grinning like an idiot, but still why the tears?'

Kelly pushed Simon into a chair and then reached around for her own, having to pull it out of the way of the passers-by. She then grabbed the magazine and thrust it in his face. He nodded, then pulled his own copy from the side pocket of his bag.

'I know. I saw it already.'

Kelly finally settled when she saw the look in his eyes and it all came swarming back to her that the whole column had been a love letter to Simon. The explanation, thanks and apology that she had not been able to put into words the week before. And that having read it, he was sitting before her. He was back just as he had promised. Just as in her heart of hearts she had known he would be.

'And what did you think?' she asked.

His mouth kicked into its most seductive grin and Kelly all but stopped breathing. 'I think that you are desperately sorry for what you have put me through this week and that as your penance you wish to grovel at my feet for ever more.'

Kelly could not help but grin back. 'Oh, you think so, do you?'

Simon leaned forward, resting his chin on one up-turned palm as he took her hand in the other, tracing the inside of her sensitive palm. 'Grovelling at my feet, bathing them, kissing the ground they walk on.'

Kelly pulled her tingling hand away as it was the only

way she would be able to continue to think straight.
'Hey, buster, that's far enough. I can take it all back,
you know.'

Simon waved the rolled up magazine in her face. 'You
can't, *you know*. It's out there. For all the world to see.
You love me. And you have accepted me back. And
whilst I have this in my hot little hand there is nothing
you can do or say to make me think otherwise.'

Kelly watched him puffing out his chest like a proud
rooster. Quick smart, she grabbed the magazine from his
hand.

He looked shocked that she had been able to do so.

'Kickboxing,' she explained, 'heightens the reflexes.'

Simon shivered. 'Remind me not to get on your bad
side.'

'Don't get on my bad side.'

He smiled again, taking her spare hand in his again,
and continuing his exploration of her palm, this time
using his soft lips to lay his claim on her responsive skin.
'Never again, sweetheart. Never, ever again.'

His eyes skimmed to clash with hers and they held.
'And I also think it was one heck of a love letter. A hell
of a lot better than the one I tried to write you. I guess
that's why you're the writer in the family and I'm the
boat-builder. I don't know any other way to say it than
that I love you too.'

'I know.' She knew but to hear it said aloud was
something else again. And she felt her fanciful heart, her
responsive body and her baffled mind fall into sync for
the first time in such a long time.

'Good. Because if you know nothing else, for ever
more, I want you to know that. Let it be your North
Star.'

'OK.'

He leaned forward and Kelly did the same and they kissed. It was light, lingering and lovely and Kelly relished every last second of it even though she knew that it was one of many more to come.

'So now what?' she asked, so full of excitement at the possibilities before her she was bouncing up and down on her chair.

'Well, I know your flatmate is not at home...'

Kelly pulled her hand away before she gave in to his tempting offer. She looked down at the rolled-up magazine in her hand, then sat up straight in her chair.

'Do you have your car?'

'I do.'

Kelly stood, wrapping Minky's leash around her wrist and grabbing Simon by the hand, dragging him from his chair.

'I need you to take me somewhere.'

'Somewhere other than your empty apartment?' he asked, pouting beautifully.

'Come on, Simon. Do as you're told.'

'Whoa. There's that bossy streak I have not seen in a long time. What have I let myself in for?' he asked, pretending to pull away from her vice grip on his hand. 'What if I want to renege? Is there a loophole through which I can back out?'

'Too late, buster,' Kelly said, her eyes alight with happiness. 'The world knows you're all mine.'

CHAPTER SIXTEEN

SIMONISM:
LOVE IS ALIVE AND WELL OUT THERE.
YOU ONLY HAVE TO LOSE YOURSELF TO FIND IT.

THEY sat in Simon's big, safe burgundy car outside the offices of *Fresh* magazine for a few minutes as Kelly gathered the fortitude to go inside. She stared up at the melon-coloured stuccoed building.

Simon rubbed softly at the back of her neck and she laid her hand on his knee. Her empty apartment was looking better and better by the second.

But, no, she had to do this first.

'I didn't think I would be coming back here,' she said.

'Why on earth not?'

'Because of that column that you so recently waved in my face like a trophy. I was waiting for my walking papers. I may still get them. The fact that it was printed does not mean that I still have a gig. But in I will go. Come on, Simon. Come be my muscle. And maybe my shoulder to cry on.'

'For the rest of time.'

Kelly felt as if she were walking the plank as she made her way across the courtyard to the front door. The only thing keeping her going was the knowledge that Simon was at her back.

Simon reached out to grab the door handle, but he

held it closed for a moment first. Kelly looked up at him in confusion.

'Hand must turn handle, to open door, to go inside,' she explained as though to a caveman.

She looked through the frosted glass door and saw movement within. She grabbed his solid hand and tugged but he wouldn't budge.

'Simon. This is hard enough already without you making it any harder.'

'Marry me,' he said.

Her tugging stilled.

'What?' she coughed, looking up at him in confusion. 'But we are already...I mean, aren't we? Did I miss something?'

'You missed nothing. But other people did. People who know us and love us missed it all. So I want to do it properly this time. With me in a proper suit and everything. Let's let your mother have the big white wedding she always dreamed for you.'

'Are you serious?'

'Absolutely. Marriage is not just about two people against the world. It's about workmates and flatmates and family and friends. It's about managing the big, wide world outside our bubble, together.'

'So this time I get to wear a white dress?'

He nuzzled against her cheek, his words blowing warm in her ear. 'Oh, I don't know about that. I thought I would go in a dinner suit and you could dust off that tiny white bikini of yours.'

'I don't think I could quite fill it out as I used to.'

Simon was close enough to glance down Kelly's zippered top to the hint of cleavage within. 'You'll do just fine.'

Kelly slapped his arm, but she was grinning from ear

to ear. 'Don't even think about it. Besides, I hear Big Bob's Rentals on Bridge Road is having a sale.'

'Well, then, how can we let Big Bob down, considering all he has ever done for us?' The corner of his beautiful mouth kicked into a slow, sexy smile as he leaned closer and closer. 'Do I take that as a yes?'

Kelly would have agreed to anything to have herself a taste of those beautiful lips. 'You bet you can.'

And taste she did. In public. On the busy city street. With all of Melbourne walking by. And from the moment his lips touched hers she forgot where she was and just sank into him, straining on her tiptoes and winding her hands around his neck.

The door was wrenched from Simon's grasp as Judy opened it from the inside. Kelly and Simon drew slowly apart. Judy was looking from one to the other, her mouth a perfect 'O'.

Simon was the first to gather himself. 'How're you going, Judy?'

The phone rang in the background and she looked over her shoulder in consternation. She turned back to Kelly. 'Maya said she wanted to see you as soon as you showed your face.'

'Well, that's just where I am heading,' Kelly said with a big smile. 'Come on, hubby, Maya wants to see me.'

Simon winked at Judy, who skulked back to answer the phone at her desk as they marched through the foyer and into the editorial room.

The white noise of the busy office stopped in an instant, like a field full of startled crickets. Kelly kept her chin high and her focus on Maya's closed door, as she knew if she saw one disappointed face she would collapse.

Then the strangest thing happened.

From nowhere Lena leapt at Kelly, enveloping her in a tight hug. 'Oh, Kelly. I am so happy for you. You have no idea. *I* had no idea. None of us did. But it's so wonderful.'

Then Kelly was swamped, surrounded by happy, excited, moist-eyed women who all hugged her tight and offered their heartfelt congratulations. Once a round of raucous applause started up Maya's office door opened with a thud.

The girls scattered back into their mouse holes as the queen cat sauntered out into the room at large.

'So, my star columnist decides to show her face.'

'Hey, Maya,' Kelly said, unable to decipher her mood. 'I wanted to introduce you to someone.'

Kelly didn't have to look over her shoulder, Simon was there in an instant, his arm slipping around her waist. He gave her a light squeeze of encouragement.

'Well, if it isn't Simon of St Kilda,' Maya said, the twinkle in her eyes the first sign of encouragement.

'This…this is my husband. I didn't tell you before because—'

Maya shushed her with a wave of her hand. 'I know why, babe. The whole country knows why, for goodness' sake. And they love it.'

Kelly hesitated. 'They do?'

'Of course they do, my sweet. You are the biggest thing in publishing right now. The agony aunt with a heart. The woman who did not believe in love falls under its spell at last. You are a shining example of hope for every incurable romantic out there. I think every woman in Australia was secretly hoping you would succumb and now they know you have they are over the moon. The phone has not stopped ringing since the damn thing hit the shelves. Readers, newspapers, current affairs TV producers. They all feel like their little Kelly has made good and they simply want us to pass on their love. This, my sweet, is going to be our biggest issue yet.'

Kelly looked around the room where all the other writers were looking at her as if she held the Holy Grail.

'So.' She swallowed. 'I guess that means I still get to keep writing for you?'

Maya cackled, startling Kelly into a fully fledged flinch. 'You bet your sweet ass you do! But rather than *Single and Loving It!* I certainly hope you can switch to *Married and Loving It!* or some such thing.' She shot a look at Simon making sure he understood that if he ever left *for milk* again he would have her to contend with as well.

Simon nodded.

Maya leaned towards the pair and said in a voice for only them to hear. 'But in order for that to happen, your story is exclusively mine, you will both be on next week's cover, and if you pull a stunt like that on me again, you will be out on that sweet ass before you can say Simon of St Kilda. Understand?'

Kelly and Simon nodded in unison.

'Well, now is probably a good time to invite you to the upcoming renewal of our vows,' Simon said. 'Perhaps you would like a *Fresh* photographer along to capture the happy day.'

Maya shot Simon a piercing look. Then she reached out and gave him a fierce pinch on the cheek. 'There's a good boy. I knew I liked this one from the start.'

She raised her voice to reach the dozens of straining ears. 'I told you this one had a grand story to tell. I can pick a good story from a mile away. That's why I am the editor and you—' she swept a hand about the room and the other writers all but cowered at their desks '—work for me.'

She disappeared back into her room but not before sending Kelly and Simon a conspiratorial wink.

The next week was a blur.

They hastily organised a dinner party at Simon's apartment. Cara and Gracie came, as did Kelly's parents. Simon's only family in town, his sister Nikki and her husband, brought their two excitable toddlers as well. Even Minky came along for the ride. As Simon intended, Kelly was surrounded by those whom she loved the most.

Cara formally met Simon for the first time and took to him straight away. Gracie had only just read Kelly's column when she met him and the poor girl burst into tears.

It seemed the Saturday Night Cocktails group was nothing but a sham. A group of mushy romantic chicks, leaning on each other until their dreams of love came true. Kelly vowed to be there for her friends in the same capacity until their day came too.

When Kelly returned to St Kilda Storeys that night she had reporters camped out on her doorstep and, in order to ensure some privacy whilst her story was still at its popularity peak, it was a stealthy trip back to Simon's, this time to stay. She'd had her fifteen minutes and then some and it was more than enough.

'Have you seen this?' Simon asked their first morning living together.

Kelly rolled over onto her stomach and shoved the pillow over her head. 'It's the middle of the night!'

'It's after nine o'clock.'

'I'm a writer,' she said, her voice muffled. 'I live by a different clock to the rest of you.'

'I've noticed. Early to bed and late to rise. I've never known anyone to sleep so long.'

'I blame you.'

'Me?'

'If you wouldn't ravage me morning and night I wouldn't be so bloody tired all the time. And then this bed, what a bed! After sleeping on a second-hand single bed all those years this is like sleeping on a cloud. I'm making up for lost time!'

She pulled her head from below the pillow to look at her husband from beneath a curtain of straggly morning hair. He was standing next to the bed holding a tray with a newspaper, a glass of apple juice and a plate with two pieces of honeyed toast.

'You are an angel, you know that? But even for an angel it's not fair that you look so gorgeous so early in the morning. You only put pressure on the rest of us.'

He sat down on the bed, pulling off the quilt, exposing her naked back to the cool morning air. 'Hey!' she screamed, whipping it back over her.

'Come on, sleepyhead, you have to see this.'

'OK,' she growled and sat up in bed, grabbing a piece of toast and chomping down. 'Read away.'

Simon read out the article from the morning newspaper. It was all about her column, no surprise there, but instead of being about her it was about her loyal readers. About the record number of marriage proposals in the week since the article had appeared. The births, deaths and marriages column in the paper had become a separate lift-out!

'I used to write those notices!' she shouted.

'I know, it says that in the article. And apparently your

biggest fan, a guy who used to insist you would one day write his obituary…'

Kelly's hand shot to cover her mouth. 'No! Is he…?'

'Engaged to be married.'

'No! Really?' She grabbed the paper from Simon's hands and devoured the words. 'I can't believe it. The old guy just knew he was going to drop any minute and now look at him.'

'I know. Planning on having the wedding of the year, or so he says.'

But he came in a far second. The wedding of the year took place a whirlwind month later, on a fresh late autumn day, in the backyard of The House in Toorak. Helicopters carrying teams of photographers roved the skies but the huge white marquee kept the ceremony and subsequent reception totally private.

Kelly's father gave her away. Her mother cried all day.

Cara played bridesmaid and official photographer. And Gracie, as maid of honour, vowed to land herself the supremely handsome groomsman, a friend of Simon's who flew over from Fremantle. Kelly didn't doubt she would succeed.

Simon's sister Kat and her boyfriend flew over from London and happily joined Nikki and family at the kiddy table with an exuberant Gillian. His mother and stepfather came over from Sydney, and they seemed really happy. They had been together for a few years and he was not letting her get away.

'Some women need to be kept on a tight rein for their own good,' Simon's stepfather confided in Kelly as they danced a lively number later in the night.

'And some men,' Kelly agreed, keeping an eye on her husband, who she knew was not going anywhere.

The celebrations lasted long into the night and Kelly and Simon had the time of their lives. They danced, they kissed, and they had eyes for only each other.

'This has been a beautiful day,' Kelly whispered into Simon's ear as he drove her back to their cosy St Kilda home.

'I'm looking forward to us having a beautiful life.'

As Kelly leaned her tired head on Simon's shoulder she smiled. 'I couldn't have written it better myself.'

Harlequin Romance®

Contract Brides

From paper marriage...to wedded bliss?

A wedding dilemma:

What should a sexy, successful bachelor do if he's too busy making millions to find a wife? Or if he finds the perfect woman, and just has to strike a bridal bargain...?

The perfect proposal:

The solution? For better, for worse, these grooms in a hurry have decided to sign, seal and deliver the ultimate marriage contract...to buy a bride!

Coming Soon to

HARLEQUIN®
Romance®

featuring the favorite miniseries Contract Brides:

THE LAST-MINUTE MARRIAGE
by Marion Lennox, #3832
on sale February 2005

A WIFE ON PAPER
by award-winning author Liz Fielding, #3837
on sale March 2005

VACANCY: WIFE OF CONVENIENCE
by Jessica Steele, #3839
on sale April 2005

Available wherever Harlequin books are sold.

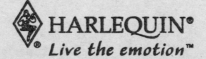

HARLEQUIN®
Live the emotion™

www.eHarlequin.com

HRCB1204

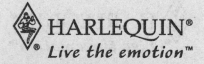

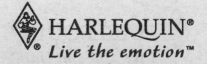

Do you like stories that get *up close* and *personal*?
Do you long to be loved *truly, madly, deeply...*?

If you're looking for emotionally intense, tantalizingly tender love stories, stop searching and start reading

Harlequin Romance ®

You'll find authors who'll leave you breathless, including:

Liz Fielding
Winner of the 2001 RITA Award for
Best Traditional Romance
(The Best Man and the Bridesmaid)

Day Leclaire
USA Today bestselling author

Leigh Michaels
Bestselling author with 30 million
copies of her books sold worldwide

Renee Roszel
USA Today bestselling author

Margaret Way
Australian star with 80 novels to her credit

Sophie Weston
A fresh British voice and a hot talent!

Don't miss their latest novels, coming soon!

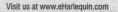

HARLEQUIN®
Makes any time special ®

The world's bestselling romance series.

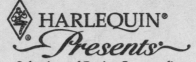

HARLEQUIN®
Presents

Seduction and Passion Guaranteed!

Back by popular demand...

EXPECTING!

She's sexy, successful and PREGNANT!

Relax and enjoy our fabulous series about
couples whose passion results in pregnancies...
sometimes unexpected!

Share the surprises, emotions, drama and suspense
as our parents-to-be come to terms with the prospect
of bringing a new life into the world. All will
discover that the business of making babies brings
with it the most special love of all....

Our next arrival will be

HIS PREGNANCY BARGAIN by *Kim Lawrence*
On sale January 2005, #2441
Don't miss it!

THE BRABANTI BABY by *Catherine Spencer*
On sale February 2005, #2450